A Kiss to Keep

Uncommon love found in an uncommon place

Vivaciousvp

This book is dedicated to my Lord, who pours out immeasurably His wisdom, strength, patience, love and long suffering. He gave me all I need to complete this assignment.

To my daughter, Kristan, who wrote two chapters of this book and Chonel, who designed the cover, I thank both of you, whom I am deeply indebted to for always helping me bring the matters of my heart and my dreams to pass.

Contents

Chapter 1

*I*N THIS DARK, SOFT silence of my mental environment, every thump of my heart continues to fall like mildewed blood that is being pumped throughout my body. *LORD! How did I get to this place,* I think. I feel septic with the fungus of heartbreak. If screaming would help, I would shout out into my hollow existence. I feel so alone and in despair. Could or would anyone try to hear me? My heart is broken, torn and worn. I don't have anything inside of me left to go on. Somebody in the Bible shouted, "Grace, grace!" to change their situation. Well, if that works, I shout, "Grace, grace, grace and more grace!" to all of my life this morning.

I lay in bed, staring at nothing in particular, and I wonder if I will ever say goodbye to my past life and I feel terrorizing fear of my future. This is not what my parents had in mind when my dad named me Bonita. Mom often told me of the beautiful, loving relationship she had with my dad. They were so in love, but he didn't marry her because he had never divorced his wife. I should have known something was wrong with that, in spite of her being my mom. Mom gets so upset when I speak of Dad's unfaithful and immoral ways. She says it wasn't him, it was the situation that life and his parents left him in. Truth be told, he did take better care of us than he did his real family and when he died, we were left a serious inheritance.

The inheritance is no comfort for Mom's heart. Loneliness continues to eat her soul to this day and the daily tears are enough to drown two cities. Those were the measurements of her emotions during my visit last year. Calling home to ask for help would break the dam because I am mother's last hope of success. She would not survive if she knew all that I have been through. This misfortune could take her over. Wasted inheritance – it would be a waste of my father's life.

Though we were left property and money, the most valuable inheritance we had was family love and the knowledge of how to be real and true. My father never accepted anything but truth from our lives. No matter how difficult truth was for him, he said that he could go anywhere with truth, no matter how much it hurt. I was in eighth grade when I had written a composition degrading my teacher. When my daddy read the essay, he was totally taken aback.

"How could his baby have written this, he asked himself in front of me.

My dad looked at me with pain in his heart and I never wanted to see that look again. Yet, at the school, he would not allow me to stand the humiliation of the consequences the principal had planned. He took me out of that school. I did have to face his consequences at home, though; I had his covering everywhere else. My dad took care of us in life and he is taking care of us in death. I wish that he was here for me to run to today.

My sister, June, from his marriage always hated me. Her mom told her many ugly stories of my parents. I felt sorry for June; she was a scorned child from a scorned mother. She always lamented that Dad took from their family to give to me. When she saw me in my new Calvin Klein outfit, she tried to tear it from my body. In return I tried to beat her brains out for touching my new clothes. We were never able to achieve friendship or even like one another.

My mind wandered around, trying to find a reason, some purpose for my situation. If Dad was here, none of this would be my reality. I was left with a greater Father who allowed a preacher husband to kick my ass, lock me in the house from dinner and curse me on the way to church. And after all of that, he would want me to smile and be the First Lady in the church. The memories of being beaten down, then picked up off the floor and expected to have passionate sex – it makes me sick. My dad would die three times if he were alive and knew of this. Thank God no children were born into that mess of a marriage.

How could I, a nurse of eight years, with an annual salary of more than eighty-five thousand dollars end up jobless, hopeless, homeless and a few other "lesses"? God, I don't feel like doing this today. The humiliation of working at the Wisdom Well Nursing home, cleaning stinking shit, changing dressings on bed sores bigger than the craters on the moon and all this medication that none of these old people need sometimes causes me to feel torn. Walking the hallways in that nursing home for what seems like pennies a day is tormenting. Just to think, the beginning of my career was heaven, this is hell on earth. I looked for a job for eight months and this is the job I landed, boy, this is desperate. The desperation continues and sometimes it seems that depression is going to win after all.

Shaking my head, I thought, Bonita you have got to get out of this slump and get moving. Depression made me tired and weak. The weight loss now totals 32 pounds. I can't go on like this. Lord somehow please give me the strength to pray. I need a way out, a breakthrough or a break off or break something. I feel me digging myself deeper into my hell at this time. "New thought pattern here please Bonita". Lord have mercy and show me my future so that I can get out of deep thought and prepare to leave for work. I want to end the struggle with the thought of fearing for my life. I have to think of a new way out this mess. Bonita got up from the bed and ran to get dressed. She had 15 minutes to get out and to get to work on time. With her head in her hands she said out loud, "These early morning pity parties have got to stop."

Jaza, Bonita screamed laughingly to her friend, "You're always happy. What happened to cause that big smile? I guess that is the product of your continuous fantasies. Never having to face reality would keep one happy. Wait a minute, maybe there is something to your way of doing life! "

Laughing across the parking deck, "we're almost late again, we have to stop this".

"We do. "

"It sounds so sweet to hear laughter roll from your heart; we have to get you out of your zone and into my fantasy life".

Jaza couldn't stop laughing. "I will not ask:" how was your night", boring I bet. Did you watch TV or just lie there again? See, you need some of my fantasy. There is a fantasy party coming up, I'm gonna bring you. "

Bonita looked at Jaza rolling her eyes. "What is a fantasy party? I guess if it makes you this happy I can't wait to get there." "Heifer "Bonita called Jaza and they laughed all the way to the time clock.

Bonita walked away smiling, but her heart was sinking. I do forgive her. She has no idea of the pain I can't recover from. It just keeps on adding on and on. Even though this job is what it is, my life breathes because of it. I don't have the drive to do anything else at this time. I found myself standing in the middle of the hallway staring into my negative abyss. Shaking of the negative, I put a smile in my heart, Jaza must be crazy getting that serious with Coffer from the internet. What kind of name is Koffer?

The morning went on uneventful. As Bonita and Carmen sat at the desk charting, Mrs. Williams made her usually trip down to the nurse's station.

"Nurse Bonita, would you be sure that I get my SeneKot tonight?

"Mrs. Williams I am sorry. Did you not get your SeneKot last night; I left a big note for the evening nurse to be sure it wasn't missed."

"I did get it, but I want to go every day. I can't miss by bowel movements. The other nurses will mess me up, Nurse Bonita. I have only you to depend on to get it right."

"I won't forget Mrs. Williams." After Mrs. Wiliams walked away Bonita turned to Carmen, "What is her fixation with her bowels." I am not sure she is not getting off".

Carmen responded in laughter, "That's a shame, I don't know if it is on her or you.

"What do you mean?"

"She is always into her bowels and you will make sure she gets what she needs. That is to get off". Both girls laughed.

෧෧

"Clocking in at 6:59 again. One day we're going to be late", Jaza chatted on. "I brought your favorite breakfast, a peanut butter and jelly sandwich, and yes, milk to drink", Jaza hands the package to Bonita.

"You should be getting ready for your wedding, not being so concerned about me. But thank you, this is my favorite", as I opened the sandwich. "So, how is your internet boyfriend"?

"How is yours, Bonita? " Jaza looked over with a big smile.

I looked at Jaza with a serious look and shouted, "Don't play". "Jaza, are you truly serious about marrying this guy you met on the internet not more than five months ago."

"Come on Bonita. Koffer is a wonderful guy. And to be real, I think it was better meeting him over the internet, he wasn't some lunatic following me around. You should meet him before you judge him. Besides, I have met so many guys and he is nothing like any of them."

"You feel safe with him. I mean, how will you really come to know him. "

"You sound so crazy, how do you get to know anyone. Does it really matter how you meet them." " Sandra's jail bird husband strangled her to death and Catrina's internet husband took her out of here to a life of luxury."

"I guess you do have a point Jaza."

Jaza looked at Bonita with an inquiring expression, "Are you curious about Koffer and I or are you asking for yourself? And besides, half the guys that are a pick up in a club have been picking up women in the club for years and is probably with someone the night he pick up the new girl. Don't let that be you".

"Girl, you're making it all sound so scary, I may never get a man."

Jaza looked at Bonita with an inquiring expression, "Are you curious about Koffer and I or are you asking for yourself?

"You've said that twice. What are you implying? I don't want an internet man."

"Where do you want to meet him"? You have no clue. I'll have to meet him for you. You say you want someone in your life but you act afraid. Don't worry, Bonita, I'm going to get you a life. Tell the truth, wouldn't you like to have a date, some dates"?

"Well, Well"

"Tell the truth and shame that devil, Bonita, would you"

"To tell the truth a good safe date would be nice. I am always one of the ladies in the restaurant sitting alone watching others with a date. Once a man sitting with his date looked at me and asked, 'Why are you beautiful sisters always eating alone? Why don't you have a man? ' I was so embarrassed. The woman with him was taking up for me.

"Not an internet date", they both laughed together. See Bonita, that is what I'm talking about. You are a young woman with your life ahead of you and you need a man. "

Walking on to the unit Bonita holding her nose laughing," This smell begins all of my weekdays. Gee whiz. Meet you for lunch Jaza. OK Lord, with you I can do this, AMEN!! Hi Kate, are you the CNA on my hall today?"

"Yes ma am."

"Did you go out drinking last night?"

"Yes ma am."

"Am I in trouble today?"

"No ma am. My boyfriend slept over last night; he got me ready for you today."

They both laughed.

Katie didn't stutter, "My linen is ready and I'm on speed dial. I have two people ready for a bath".

"Don't do any decubitus care on patient's until after... "

"After your med pass, Katie completed Bonita's sentence. " I was 30 minutes early and some of my patients are up with am care completed. I have this, Boo,"

Bonita looked at her with both excitement and amazement, "damn your man is good. Does he have an uncle? Hold up. You met him on the internet too, didn't you?"

Bonita gave Kate a big hug. "Give him a hug for me too girl." Bonita looked at Kate with a serious encouraging stare, "I am so proud of you. I don't know too many people who could have done it like you did. You are my champion."

Katie filled with hope and encouragement. Her heart beat with joy, "Ms. Bonita, thank you and a million smooches cause I could not have done it without your encouragement. And no, no woman gets to hug Mike Jike but me"

"I'm beginning to believe Mike Jike the mystery man is not real."

"See how I'm workin". As they walked from the assignment board, Kate said, "Ms Bonita, can I have lunch with you today".

Bonita sighed and said, "OK, I know what a lunch date with you means.

Chapter 2

*T*HE MORNING WAS MONOTONOUS, as most days were. On days her good boyfriend spent the night, Kate was on automatic and that day, she worked like a busy bee. The patients were ecstatic because she was overboard with attention towards them. Mrs. Jackson seemed happy because Kate sat with her, reading from the one book her deceased husband had written. Everyone on the ward had that book memorized. Sometimes, they all had to sit through an unannounced memorial service for Mr. Jackson because if they didn't, Mrs. Jackson would become catatonic. Once, she laid there for three and a half days, and they all thought they would lose her.

At times, they let off steam by talking negatively with one another about the clients in the facility, but Bonita knew that they all saw the patients as family. They were all one big family. It is almost as if they had been with the patients throughout their lives. Bonita knew she was not the only person who felt as if she had known Mr. Johnson personally. Before she died, she thought it would be great to experience a love affair like the one Mr. and Mrs. Johnson shared. They laughed, fought and cried with all of their clients, but it is so painful for the staff when it is time for one of them to go on to the next life. The Wisdom Well would become the House of Grief.

"Last night, you were complaining about Mrs. Jackson. I believe you have come to love the clients, Kate, and they love you back. I see Mrs. Jackson and her gang are ecstatic because you are officiating the memorial again today. Are you having lunch today, girl?"

"This place and all of us are all they have Bonita. I do like them and your feelings are not hidden under your bed. If one of the clients says 'ouch,' you go running towards them."

"They are my honey bunches of oats," Bonita said, with a gentle smile. "You should return to the memorial of the Mr. Samson Jackson before his widow falls out into a catatonic state again. But, if you cry again while reading the obituary, I will laugh and call everyone to see. You are crazy, Kate. "

"Ms. Bonita, I'm trying to get a husband. I can't imagine being married for 62 years to the same man and wake up one morning to find him dead. He went to sleep, laughing and talking after he had prepared the food and music for the picnic in their backyard for the next morning and he woke up dead."

"Girl, stop it," Bonita laughed. "I get it Kate. Will you have the opportunity to go to lunch?"

"I can't leave her like this."

"Kill me dead before I listen to that story again. Rock 'em, sock 'em dead!" Bonita laughed. "Deliver her, dear Jesus. Ok, then, I'll have a quiet lunch today. Maybe we can have lunch together tomorrow."

"Ok. Glad you understand."

Kate walked sadly back into Mrs. Johnson's room.

Looks like I'll be eating from the vending machine today. What is low calorie? I can't go for anyone else's life sucking moments at this time, Bonita thought. *Thank God for Kate and her patience with Mrs.*

Johnson. Lord Jesus, help me, please. Here I go, mind bowling. Knock that thought down.

Bonita laughed out loud and walked down the hall.

I will not be Sad Bonita today, she thought, as she fought the negative imaginations.

"Bonita, I didn't know this was your lunchtime. They didn't put me on your hall today."

"Happy to see you, Jaza."

"Please tell me you are not having one of your pity parties today. Are you ok?"

"Kate is working hall two with me today and her boyfriend slept over last night. She is going to cause a strain in that man's groin. But, I am ecstatic to have her helping me."

"I hate when she works with you because you don't miss me. Good for Kate. I wish something was hittin' me like that. Has she chosen which one yet?"

Bonita laughed. "What about Koffer? He doesn't hit it that good? Be sure that is right before you marry him."

"We not hittin' it like that yet. He says we are going to Christian date, no sex before marriage. And besides, if I find someone to do that with, he will leave me, then this job will be my end."

"No, Jaza, this job will never become your end. Please don't tell me you need to go join the memorial service. Your report is that you're Boaz and you are doing fine."

"My man is doing fine. I can feel that he has quite a stick on him. Kate's got two guys that want to marry her. She is bound to be out of here soon. The truth is, I hate this job. There has to be something. Two men together does pay the rent. I think about that sometimes when Koffer gets his holy moments."

"What, Jaza? Lord Jesus. I don't think it is any of our dreams to work here. Be encouraged. This is a means to an end. Think of Koffer and his special gifts he laid on you. You'll be alright. Work on the wedding plans and make it legal. I'll be the maid of honor."

"Wouldn't be a wedding if you were not the maid of honor. Bonita, I'm scared about the marriage and what is going on here at the Well. I have seen a few new faces around the Wisdom Well. I am not sure what is going on, but there are strange things in the air. I don't know what is in store for us."

"You are concerned about the job you hate," Bonita said, amusedly. "Be on your job so that you won't have to be afraid."

"You had to go there, right!"

"The fear you are feeling is good. This may be the situation that separates you from this job and enables you to become your own person. Jaza, this place does not define you and is not your source. It is only a job, hear me. You have a wonderful guy and now have a promising life ahead. Leaving here would be a giant step to bigger and better. Besides, you have a wedding to plan. If I had something like that going on in my life, I would not be thinking of all these old cronies. You already have mother-in-law problems. And Kate, she doesn't have it better. If she loved either guy enough to marry, the other one would not still be a choice. It is no such thing that you have to put two guys together to make one."

"You think Koffer is so wonderful. I haven't told you the whole Koffer story."

Bonita's eyes filled with fear. "I've told you over and again about those Internet guys! Lord have mercy!"

"It's not the Internet guy, it is the Internet, girl."

"Girl, we will have to talk. I'm scared of the look in your eyes, but I think Koffer is the fire to this new attitude you have. You are not looking for another guy on the Internet, are you? What is going on? I am confused now."

With a face full of a smile and tears, Jaza sighed before speaking.

"I am glad to have met him. I think guys are as afraid to meet us as we are to meet them. But, you know what, Bonita? In the end,we all just want to be loved."

"You could be so right," Bonita said. "What is going on? Is there someone else? I'm feeling something deeper."

"Bonita, I believe in my heart that you would like to have a man in your life."

"What the hell? We are not talking about my empty bed. If I had someone that wanted to marry me, I would take him to the Justice of the Peace. Then, I would call this job and quit."

"Girl, I am going to get you a man before you're old and dried up. If I don't find a guy for you, someone is going to have to get you some female Viagra by the time you get a man," Jaza said, with a giggle.

"I will kill a man because he is going to have to pay me back for all the time I am without. He will need Viagra, Cialis, a pump and an implant."

"Wow. I'm going towork on some sleeping partners for you. One man's heart cannot take all –"

"I don't have casual sex. Back up. Not a guy from the Internet. I don't think so. I'm not playing with you," Bonita responded with her hands on her hips. "You can't be serious."

"More serious than that code you ran last week. As a matter of fact, I – well, you – met a guy on the rightonemeetup.com. I can make arrangements for you guys to meet on a double date with Koffer and me sometime soon," Jaza said, with a smirk.

"Don't play, Jaza. What do you mean?! I'm not going on dates with a computer man! Sounds like that song, 'Computer love.' That is not and will never be my reality."

"This is not your reality or your world. This is my fantasy and you invited yourself in. Stop being so stuck up Bonita. Let loose and live."

"What have you done?"

"Why do you look as if you are about to cry? It is not that serious. Please! You must need to talk cause this is not that serious."

"Jaza, I'm not ready for any of this. There are too many things that I cannot face at this time. The real Bonita was murdered and I am not ready to die all over again."

"Just in time, here comes the New Orleans preacher himself, the Wisdom Well's own Pastor. Hi, Lloyd," Jaza chuckled.

"Hi, Lloyd," Bonita said, with a surprised expression. "I didn't know you were a pastor."

Jaza hit Bonita in the side with her elbow, and then said, "That girl plays too much."

Bonita looked around, wondering what was going on. "Are you working today?"

"Feeding tube alley," Lloyd replied. "What are you two up to?"

"Nothing," Jaza said. "I was just telling Bonita how you were a good listener and helping other coworkers out when they were going through something."

"If that's why ya'll call me Pastor, I don't mind. Do you think I don't know what ya'll say about me? It is all good and I am proud of my reputation with you ladies. It would be nice to have a few other males on my side. That's what it is all about, right? I am not ashamed of the gospel of Jesus Christ. Are you having some problems, Bonita?

"Not at all, Lloyd. What would make you think that?" Bonita felt herself fighting back tears. "Jaza was just telling me what a great guy you are."

"Actually we were discussing my fiancée, whom I met on the Internet. If Bonita was Catholic, she would think that I committed a mortal sin and she'd send me past Purgatory and straight to hell."

"Sin," Lloyd laughed. "If she was Catholic, I would have committed the mortal sin also. I met my wife on the Internet two and a half years ago. I had been praying for a good woman for a long time and the Lord gave me my good thing from the Internet. All of the women in church are looking for a church man to take care of them. And all of the other good women were home praying for a man 'cause they didn't want to be associated with men from the club. Sooo, I had to find a way to get to the women in the prayer closet who were waiting for her Godly man to come get her. I love the Lord and I love my Internet wife."

Jaza looked at Bonita with a 'see there' look, and Bonita looked at Lloyd with a feeling of suspicion.

"You truly believe that, don't you," Bonita asked, staring at Lloyd with a pout on her face.

"I am glad I had faith enough to believe it and now, I am living it. I knew from our first conversation that she was mine. I told her the first time we met that she was my wife. She thought I was some sort of freak. Her mom and her whole family had copies of my driver's license, license plate number and all of my info. I laughed at them and six months later, we were married."

"How is your marriage now?" Bonita asked suspiciously.

"Wonderful. Absolutely wonderful. I have never been happier in my grown life. We are asking God for a baby at this time; pray with us. But, that doesn't seem to be what's really bothering you, Bonita. What's really wrong?"

"Don't try to read me. I really can't appreciate that."

"Read you? Baby, witches do that," Lloyd replied gently. "But, if God shows me something, I will let you know. In the meantime, I will be praying for peace in your heart."

Bonita stood looking at Lloyd, stunned that he could say those things to her.

Lloyd turned to Jaza and asked, "How are you and your Internet man?"

"Great! He seems more excited about me every time we talk and meet. He makes my heart so happy. Even if he is not the right thing to do, I'm going to enjoy him while I have him."

"That is no way to begin your relationship. Pray. The Lord will never steer you wrong and if this man is for you, He will sign, seal and deliver it. You must believe and encourage your man. Take that advice from this man because it is what we need."

"Well, maybe you should give Bible study at lunch or something. We all can use some prayer and wisdom."

Bonita pondered on Lloyd's words that were pounding against her mind throughout the rest of the day and his words served as her meditation throughout the night. As she lay alone in bed, she admitted to herself that she had not allowed herself enough time to deal with her broken heart and all the pain and abuse from my past.

∾

"Good Morning."

The silence from no response made her look harder. Lloyd and the new girl were standing holding hands. Bonita was sure he told her about his wonderful wife. *What's up with this?*

Lloyd looked over and spotted Bonita staring.

"Would you like to pray with us?" he asked her.

Bonita did not answer that question because she was about to pray anytime soon. She remembered the days in church with her ex-husband and leading women's prayer all too well; it was more memory than she wanted to care about at this time. The only way out of this holy-rolling conversation was to change the subject. She looked to the new nursing assistant and introduced herself.

"This is Judy," Lloyd said. "I worked with her at a previous job. The politics is the same on every job, isn't it?"

Kate walked up at that moment and said, "You guys still here talkin'? The night crew will tell. We best go to our place of abode for today. Lloyd, lead us females."

"Good morning, Nurse Sigrid," Bonita greeted as she stepped onto the unit.

"Why am I not surprised that you are working this unit again? I went to Mrs. Stanzer about that issue."

"What issue? Should we get into report before we start talking about this, Sigrid?"

"Report is report. Nothing has changed. Someone should get a fever or a cough or something. Anything that would give me something to do."

"You're right. Ok, what's up and why did you go to Mrs. Stanzer? Everyone is talking about strange things going on. I see Kate is here with me today and she is on her roll, so I can talk a minute."

"I went to Mrs. Stanzer about you and I having to work this unit continuously. I am working too hard. Sundown syndrome is roaring. Five a.m. med pass have to start at four am because it is so much. I'm tired and we need a break. That is what I told her."

"I'm so tired, I am numb, Sigrid. Numb about a whole lot of things. But, some days, all of this work is therapy for me."

"That is what she is banking on. Her words to me were that 'you don't complain and you're a registered nurse doing the job of a licensed practical nurse, so why is the LPN complaining?'"

Bonita could feel Sigrid staring at her as she waited for her response. She could tell that Sigrid needed to hear that she would back her up.

"What did you say?"

"I told her it was because you were too tired to complain. Aren't you? We should go storm her office right now."

"Please, Sigrid. I respect you more than I respect anybody else around here, but I will not waste my time on the petty situation at hand. Someone has to take care of these people. Look, Sigrid, I got through nursing school by reading with a flash light in the closet. Dragged to bed at night and dragged out of bed in the morning. The old people on this unit can't talk. Just do it how you want to and love them."

"Bonita, I am afraid to ask you what you are talking about, so I'll leave it alone."

"If I told you my story, you would be afraid. Did you make any coffee this morning? I love your coffee."

"Yeah, Lloyd went home to New Orleans and bought back some CDM coffee with chicory."

"New Orleans coffee is the best. Sigrid, did you know he met his wife on the Internet?"

"No, I didn't know that. Quite a few people around here are dating or married to someone from the Internet. I know his wife is a wonderful lady. I have met her. They give a prayer brunch at their home four times a year. It has been a while since the last one; the next one should be coming up soon."

"You and I don't have a personal relationship, Sigrid, but we do have a nurturing relationship. You comfort me when you don't know you are. Some days during these last three weeks, I did not have the strength to move and get out of bed. Maybe God has us here together so that you would care for me. Do you think those Internet relationships are good? Do you think that I am a transparent person?"

"I didn't know you felt that way about me. Thank you, Bonita. The one strong asset you bring to my life is building focus. You talk from one subject to another in the middle of a sentence. It is a little scary that I keep up and understand you. Back to what you are asking – just because a couple met on the Internet doesn't make it an Internet relationship. The Internet is just the coincidental meeting place. That is merely where they happened to meet. You do not look like the weak type. If I could do all that for you, I am so glad."

"The nurse Lloyd from New Orleans told me he knows that I am going through something and have a lot on my mind. When the Lord gives him something to tell me, he would let me know."

"Um... That nurse has helped a lot of people around here. So, you were bothered by what he said?"

"Why do you say that?" Bonita asked.

"Our relationship may not be hanging together outside of the job, but I have been in your presence enough to know when something is bothering you. But, to answer your real question, you were not that transparent, that is until now. "

"Until now. Now, I have to face my past so that I can live my present and have a future. Sigrid, it is very complicated. I pray that the sins of my father fall on his other children. Thank God the Bible doesn't speak about the sins of the mother because I am her only child. I have all of my past issues to deal with; I can't handle other people's."

Without realizing it, Bonita began to chatter on to Sigrid. She became lost in her thoughts.

"When he knew his days were coming to an end, my dad set my life up with a preacher man whose mother was looking for a wife for him. He thought that would be security for my life and assurance to him that I would be well taken care of when he was gone. Nope, not so. After my dad died, that man beat my brains out, raped me and tortured me every chance he got. But, to the church, he was their hero. His mom gave me the idea and I developed a three-year great escape. I wish I had known how to live my own life and make decisions because I would not have followed my dad's choices in my life for a man he thought was great to marry. I don't know because my dad surely was not a husband to his married family, but that was his story. Sigrid, when I raise my head to go on from one situation, my past memories and another situation always stares me in my face. How can I go on?"

Sigrid was quiet for a moment before speaking. "I thought the fact that we are not rotating and you have to work this unit so often was why you were upset. I feel embarrassed."

"Well, Sigrid, I see you are preoccupied with caring for the wonderful people on this unit. Get past it, Sigrid. Didn't you notice no one is rotating anymore? Without saying it, she has assigned us to permanent units."

"I didn't notice that, Bonita. How did you know that?"

"I pay attention, Sigrid."

"You have so much hanging on your heart, Bonita. The one thing I do know is that the past doesn't matter much. Review once more and take out the things that you need from it and hold it dear to you, then throw the rest away and move on."

"Move on. I want to be married with children, but every time I think about a man, I think about the mates that my father and husband were"

"Your father, was he mean to your mother?" Sigrid asked.

"In no way. My father had extreme love for my mother and me. He took meticulous care of us. It was the woman he was married to and her children that I felt bad for. He gave them just enough money and himself for them to survive. How he started there, I don't know, but he ended up with us. My mom didn't bury him; she said that was for his wife to do. And that is what has puzzled me all this time. It did not matter how much he did for us, there were some things my mom would not do. When there was something that she wouldn't do, she'd send him to his wife. Those times did hurt my father badly." Bonita paused and sighed. "Alright, enough about me and my sick past. Let's get back to this place."

"I don't know what is going on around here, Bonita. New faces are roaming and no one has been introduced. It is almost as if a new community within a community is being developed. We have no input, but we have not been put out yet. The not knowing is scary."

"All I know, Sigrid," Bonita said, sadly. "is that I will not be able to take being shafted on another job. I know I need this job to survive right now, but I have made a lot of sacrifices for these people and this place."

"Bonita, look at me." Sigrid took Bonita's hand in hers. "Give none of what you have done for these old people's lives to the credit of this place. Give it all to the glory of God. He is the only one who will repay you fairly. Believe me, I have been there." Then, Sigrid gently brought her hand to Bonita's face and said, "You're going to have to share all of the weight on your heart with someone."

"You're right, Sigrid. Do you remember the time Mr. James chewed the double mint gum and got it caught up in his false teeth? He pulled at that gum throughout the entire church service trying to get it off. " Both nurses fell down laughing, remembering the event. "I had to pull the gum out with hemostats.

"That is what I am trying to do with my past troubles except I can't laugh all the time. I guess there is no place like this place," Bonita said, catching her breath. "Maybe Nurse Lloyd will get a word for me from God. That is a quote of his."

"Yes, he is prophetic!" Sigrid said.

"What does that mean?"

"He hears from God, God speaks things to him to help others lives."

"Oh. That is a little deep right now for me, Sigrid."

"Bonita, I'm past my time to leave. Have a great day. I am going to be praying for you and praying for us to rotate off this unit."

"No, don't pray that for me. Pray for me to get a real RN job."

"I understand," Sigrid said, as they hugged.

"Enjoy your coffee." Kate called out. "Everybody is up and a.m. care is complete and ready for medication and breakfast. I have your medicine cart set up for you; it is ready to go."

Chapter 3

"WHAT WAS SERVED IN the cafeteria that caused everyone to have diarrhea?" Bonita asked. "We have cleaned more shit today than a sewer in New York could hold in a month's time. When you get home, take your clothes off at the door and take a bath. We have to wash all of this off of us. I hope it is not viral because we'll be cleaning ourselves tomorrow."

"That was the most potent poo poo I have ever had to smell," Kate moaned. "I cleaned my nostrils out with alcohol to get rid of the smell. Did you ever see Mr. Thomas down there? That man is hung like a horse."

"I would not want anything that big going in me. That is unreal. That's not the treat, the Mr. Man, Mr. Castile. His old lady lives here."

"I know who ain't got nothin' to talk about."

"Say no more. The doctor ordered him to be catheterized once and I need a hemostat to find his penis."."

"You found it; we should call you Bonita the Miracle Worker. I thought he didn't have a dick. My heavens, what is his wife runnin' around here thinkin' someone is gonna get?"

"She should stop accusing other women," Bonita said. "Someone is going to cuss her out and accuse her of being a fantasy writer. But, I have seen him around here."

"Me too, but considering the ages, I can imagine he might use –"

"Enough said, Kate. Too deep envisioning"

"Ok, I won't talk about it anymore. I'm tired."

"Clean up and eat a good diner, in that order. You didn't have lunch today."

"You didn't either, Bonita. We both are hungry."

"I don't feel up to cooking either. I may go to bed from the bathtub. That way, I don't have to think."

"That's not good, Bonita. I'll see you tomorrow. I need to talk with you. Maybe we can talk then."

The drive home for Bonita was slow. Traffic was thicker than mud sludge. Bumper to bumper. She figured there might have been an accident and, sure enough, she passed by a six car collision. When she arrived home, she got undressed at the front door and showered immediately. Her mind was too full to think. This was her first relaxing moment of the day.

She got out of the shower, dressed in comfortable clothes and let herself sink into the couch. Just as she shut her eyes, the phone rang. Just as she suspected, it was Kate.

"Hello?"

"Hi, girl."

"Hello Kate, is everything ok?"

"Everything is good. I was hoping that you would meet me for dinner since we missed lunch."

Bonita contemplated her relaxing shower and sat quietly on the phone, thinking that she felt too restless to sleep and needed something new instead of wallowing about loneliness and depression.

Kate said, "Aw, come on, I know whatcha thinkin'. You rest every evening."

"If the place you've chosen is motivating, I will come. Will there be dancing and can I get a glass of wine or two or three? Where do you want to meet?

"At the Cast Iron Skillet, the meal is on me. I need to talk."

"Cast Iron Skillet? Ok."

Hope this is not overwhelming. Kate's talks can put the hurt on me, she thought.

"I'll be waiting. 6:30," Kate said.

Kate was excited to meet with her; that was obvious to Bonita when she arrived. They walked into the establishment and immediately onto the dance floor. Bonita let herself go and she was dimly aware of the fact that Kate had never seen her this way. Bonita didn't mind, though, and she rocked out to every song. The DJ even left the booth to dance with her. He came up and greeted her, saying, "Hi, Diane." Kate gave them some space and went to find a table. After a few dances, he bought Bonita a glass of wine. They spent a couple of songs talking over the music. After a while, she excused herself and went to find Kate.

Kate looked at her and smiled. "I'm not gay, but you look so beautiful!"

"If you were gay, you would be working pretty hard to cover up."

They both laughed loudly, then fell into a heavy quiet.

"Have you ordered?" Bonita asked Kate

"I ordered a drink, but waited for you to order food."

"I hope you ordered another glass of Riesling because I want to go home and pass out. Is there a limit to what I can order?"

Kate laughed at Bonita and said, "Don't forget, I am a nursing assistant. You are a nurse and we have to work in the morning."

"No, I don't think so. Let's call out. We both can use the rest, considering the length of time we have worked our unit. Perfect excuse: diarrhea."

"Girl, I never thought I would hear this from you. Ok then. If you do it, I'll do it."

The ladies ordered and Kate said, "Bonita, I just want to thank you so much. I would not be here if it were not for you. I am so grateful."

"Oh, come on, Kate. Life deals us hard hands all the time. Only the strong survive. You had to be strong within yourself. You are the reason you survived. And besides, we met in a homeless shelter."

"You were in the homeless shelter and took me in; I was on the street. Bonita, you have been there throughout many tough struggles, from the bottom to a place of self-confidence and home. The struggle to survive after drug addiction, my pimp's abuse and homelessness was overwhelmingly murderous and I felt like I would have died a while ago, but then came Bonita. You encouraged me to face my fears. If you had not been there to encourage me, to stop me from self-destruction I would have overdosed. I wanted more drugs and you gave me hope. You walked me to the clinic, walked me to the school and tutored me through homework. For six weeks, you did that every day. I did not get to say that I appreciate you until now. I have something exciting to tell you. I did talk with my grandma weekend past."

"Kate, that is so wonderful. There is nothing better for me to hear. Thank you, Jesus."

"Right, thank you, Jesus. I don't know Jesus, but I say 'thank you' anyway. Mom wanted to hear and I told her all about my life, my job and you. I told her I had a future planned. Bonita, my mom cried. She sobbed. She told me to tell you thank you. She asked me if I wanted to come home. But, of course, I told her no. Since you taught me to lean on my own strength, going home could make me weak. Mom said to go see about furthering my education; she is going to pay for it. I agreed to go home to visit. I would have none of this if it were not for you."

Bonita looked at Kate with tears in her eyes. Overjoyed, she exclaimed, "Kate, I am so happy for you. I am so happy. I didn't do anything. You now have the life. God knows who He made you and came to pick you up and put you on that track."

The two talked about Kate's life and future over dinner. It was a good evening with rewarding conversation. Then, Kate's expression changed and she said, "There is something I need to speak with you about."

In the midst of all of her accomplishments, what could be wrong? Bonita has had to pull her out of pits previously, drag her from the pusher's car and pay the pusher for her life. God has allowed so much change. Kate is the most loving, caring nurse's assistant I have ever known. What could be the matter at this time in her life?

"What's up, Kate? I am listening."

"I am scared, Bonita. I'm so scared."

"What is going on? What are you afraid of?"

"I am afraid of life, Bonita."

Bonita relaxed. She understood that life, especially when you have come back from the dead, can be too much sometimes. The reality of every day can be consuming. She knew she had to put on her hat of compassion. "I am listening Kate. Go ahead. "

"Why did you tell the DJ your name is Diane?"

"What? Because I don't know him and I live alone. I can't make it easy for strange men to get to me. But, I am sure that has nothing to do with the reason we are here. I told him I know where to find him when I want to see him."

"See him."

"No, that's just an expression. You never know guys and when they might hurt you."

"I have my job, my apartment is a home and I am doing the right things. I am not tempted by drugs. I do drink alcohol sometimes," Kate said. "I know I am not supposed to, but I do. I know you told me be careful about relationships. You told me I need to get me together before I try to have me and someone else. I am afraid of being alone. I am uncomfortable with everything going well. I am afraid of my mom being proud and loving me. It would be less stressful if I'd go back to the life I was used to. Never do I want to be on the street selling myself again, but nobody expected anything from me but the worst. Bonita, I don't want to go back. Help me."

Kate looked as if she was going to cry and Bonita moved over to her seat and held her hand tightly.

"Many days, I feel like running. Where, I don't know. My pain continues to hold me prisoner," Bonita told Kate. "I live in the fear of my past daily after work, the prison of heartbreak and brokenness is mine. I am so familiar with what you are feeling. Where do we go from here, Lord?"

Bonita held Kate's face in her hand, much like Sigrid had done for her because that brought her such comfort.

"Kate, you are not the things you have done. My past is not perfect, either. Lord, wrong decisions landed me in that homeless shelter a rape victim and pride keep me there. But, the dreams of God came and got us out. It's a process for all of us and we are still in the mist of our process. We must learn to make our pain work for us, stop holding onto pain; it is not our security. Pain is not the only experience you have had in life. We do have good things in our past life to think on. It will give you the energy to remove yourself from the pain. You will see the pain is not good. But, you will hold on to the good the pain produced. It will all be over in a minute. The worst of it all has past. You've got to let go of the pain of the past. Your past pains are eating your today and your future when it should be its fertilizer. You've got to try to imagine all of your dreams as a reality, Kate."

Kate looked at Bonita like she was on another planet.

"Bonita, woman, you know my reality, what are you talking about? What am I supposed to think or do when I'm craving dope, Bonita? My reality is that I stood on the street, selling sex so that I could survive tomorrow. I was so high in places I didn't even know where I was.

I was raped and abused. Somehow, I am still living. I think I am sane, but I don't know for sure."

"That was a long time ago, Kate. That insanity is all gone. Take the gain from the bad experiences. Shake the rest of that off and leave it behind. You have to cross too many great experiences to get to the ugly. Butterfly, you are not a worm anymore. Kate, this morning, as I sat at my kitchen table, I thought about the universe. God created the universe and from all of the planets, He chose one that was fit for human life. He placed us on the outside of this round ball and we did not fall because of gravity. He had wisdom to create gravity to hold us on the earth. And that same God has the wisdom to hold you on your new earth."

"Bonita, what the hell does that have to do with this conversation? That is not what I need right now."

"This is exactly what you need at this time and hell is mad because you've got it now."

"Ok, what then?"

"All of that is to change your way of thinking, know who created you."

"God, ok."

"It was an endless mind that created you. You are going to have to change what you are thinking. If you do not deal with you, you will continue to go around the same mountains."

"You and your examples. What are you saying to me?"

"I am saying you will need to change what you are thinking. Take from your past only the things that can grow your future. Girl, I can understand that you don't know how to live life, think what it is that would make you happy, what you want. Remember the girl that you were before the tragedy. That is not the only life you had. Remember your hopes and dreams. Remember the dreams that your grandma had for you. Yes, your life did get off track, but you have discovered the Kate road again. I will help you apply to school. I know this job has been your miracle. There are greater miracles to come."

"You don't understand! It is not that easy. You don't understand at all."

"I understand more than you think. What made you do drugs and what is on your mind when you crave for them now? But, it is the thoughts that keep you from going back and the love of your boyfriend that sustains you. In the beginning and the end, it is all about love. And love don't come the way we think it should. Never."

A few moments of silence went by and Bonita noticed tears trickling down Kate's face. "We are going to crash this mountain now. I need you to say it."

Bonita moved closer to Kate because she knew that this subject continued to be an emotional burden for her and did not want to draw attention. In the back booth of the restaurant, the two girls ignored the stares because Kate needed freedom from her past. She realized the promising future ahead for Kate and also understood that Kate's past obscured her from seeing the greater future evolving on her life's horizon.

"Now is the time for you to stop your past from blackmailing you from –"

"My mother, mother," Kate cried. She looked up into Bonita's eyes with a look of grief and death, "He didn't have to kill her, Bonita. He cut her apart. He left me with no chance of knowing her. Those thought of her lying there terrorize me day and night. I need something to make me forget. My grandmother told me her stories over and again, so that I would hate him and all black people. My mother is dead and my sister's father killed her."

Tears fell from both of their faces; Bonita held her hand and prayed. When dinner arrived, they ate and reminisced on Kate's past life dreams. They laughed and moved on to have a joyous time.

Suddenly, Kate looked up at Bonita and said, "He says he loves me and wants to marry me. How can I trust him not to hurt me?"

"You can't put your trust in him because he is human. Something in your lifetime together will hurt you. Your heart's preparation for his humanism will stop you from developing scars and becoming bitter. You will have to trust God. The same God that brought you out will bring you through. Trust God to keep you and him. Which guy is it? I only know Mike Jike and that is not his real name. Do I know him?"

"His name is Josiah. Mike Ike and Josiah is the same person. There is only one guy."

"His name is Josiah, but we talk like he is two guys. Ok, we won't discuss the fact of one guy with two names; too much at this time. "

The conversation went on about Josiah for about another hour. Kate set plans and goals for her future and said she would discuss the plans with Josiah later. When it was time to part, Kate put her head down and asked Bonita, "You really think all of this can happen?"

"I know it can. I don't like that the night, rather morning, has to come to an end, but it is time to go. We will have to bring the other girls to this place. I had a good time. Do you want to sleep over to my house tonight? It might be good for both of us. This conversation did cause me to rehash some of my own personal heartbreaks and past nightmares."

"No, Bonita, I am sorry," Kate said. "I feel like I have power right now. I'll talk to Josiah tonight until I fall asleep. Hey, before we go, I didn't tell you one thing. The reason I talked about Josiah as two people and didn't let anyone meet him is because he is black."

"OK then!" Bonita said. "That caught me off guard. I understand that being an issue with your grandma and family. You do know that will take the wind from under your grandma's wings. To everyone else, that is no case or point."

"White boys don't like me. They abuse me. I don't want to go that way anymore. He really likes me; I think he loves me, Bonita. He treats me with respect. He has never asked me for anything. When he met me, I was on the corner, trying to make a hustle. He took me home, cleaned me up and told me not to do that anymore. Though I did, he loved me through it all."

"That love is what makes his race null and void in your heart, Kate?"

"My grandfather always warned me about black guys. My sister's dad was black and you remember what he did to my mother. If I married a black guy, my grandfather would not ever speak to me again. My grandfather would not be disgraced with such a person in our family. That's why my mom moved away from her family. My grandfather loved my mother, but his shame and pride separated them. After mom was murdered, my grandparents refused to raise my sister. What are people going to think?"

"Who cares what people think? When you speak with your grandfather again, refer to Josiah as Mike Jike. He will come to love him like I did. Once he loves him, it will be hard to hate him. Are you going to say to God, 'Thank You for the gift, but you sent the wrong color?' If someone gave you a black Mercedes and you always wanted a red one, would you give it back or hide it in a corner? Certainly not. Maybe God is bringing healing through your relationship with Josiah. Who knows the mind of God? I would say enjoy it."

Chapter 4

*A*NGER CREATED A BURNING inferno against the walls of Bonita's brain and heart that disseminated throughout her body. She held onto her scorched hair and scalp so that her head wouldn't blow off, and she kept her mouth sealed tight because she felt like anyone on the other side of her breath would be charred by her dragon fire. She was mad and someone would experience her anger today.

Bonita met Jaza on her way into work the next morning.

"Good morning," Bonita said. "This will not be a good day for me. I did not forget my past, but today I am going to build warfare for my future. I will not be the victim any longer, Jaza. I am going to sit here, drinking my coffee while devising a strategy for war. I feel like I can explode remembering all the experiences I had to complete school and that gives me the fire needed to accomplish this mission. Having to work a LPN position to keep from being homeless and starving was not easy and no one told me about an RN position here in this nursing home. How dare they bring an RN to work over me?! This won't go down smoothly, not this day."

"Bonita, I can see the fury flowing from your pores. Calm down, calm down. She is in training. She may not work this facility. She is training. Her name is Mrs. J. Wash."

"I know the witch. Not that wicked dog," Bonita growled."

Carmen ran to Lloyd for help.

"Dealing with my personal animosities are enough and I understand Bonita's explosive behavior towards this woman. I resent that Mrs. Wash showed up on this job. I ask myself if this pig had searched for the two of us to bring more torment to our lives. "

"Calm down, Carmen. We will get together to discuss what's going on. Keep walking, I am following you. You're beginning to speak in Spanish and I don't understand your language. I am sorry, but calm down. "

Jaza looked in amazement. "Bonita, I have never seen you in such a stage of rage."

At that time, Carmen walked up with Steven. She looked at Jaza, then Bonita and said, "I see you've heard."

"I am not understanding what I have heard," Jaza said. "What the hell is going on?!"

Carmen screamed softly between her teeth, "That woman is more than a bitch."

"Oh my God, I got that! I don't want to know anymore. Who is this woman and where did she come from?"

Lloyd stood there silently while the ladies continued to speak bitterly. After they quieted, he looked calmly at Bonita and said, "It will not happen here like it happened before."

Bonita looked at Lloyd with a confused expression. "What?"

"Purpose has been served and it will not happen like it happened before," he said.

Carmen began to weep quietly. She later claimed that stress was getting to her, that she had a headache and was feeling dizzy. She ended up going home for the remainder of the day.

On Unit Two, Bonita was unable to focus. She sat at the desk, doing nothing throughout the remainder of the shift. Being caught off guard made the war bigger than Bonita could have imagined. Kate managed the unit until 3:15 when relief came.

୦୨

Bonita rushed out in great dismay. She raged alone all the way home.

To hell with this shit, she thought. *If these heifers think they will... This will not happen to me like this. I have poured my all into this place. I'll be damned if I get fucked like this again. No way. Mrs. Stanzer laughed with me and treated me like I was the best nurse she had working at that home. She repeatedly said I am her gift from God. So, how could she? Lord, I don't think you can hear or see any of this because this cannot be happening to us again.*

Bonita was blind with anger, and she dodged in and out of traffic. The cars on the road continued to dodge her avoiding accidents. When Bonita looked up, she had driven to the lake, the place she did came to on the day Mrs. Wash fired her and the place she came often for peace. There, she sat and sobbed until it was dark.

Mrs. Wash had been Bonita's worst nightmare, as well as for Carmen and a few other nursing staff members. Never could she have imagined working with this woman again. How could a living God have allowed this to happen?

Unbelievable, this is unbelievable.

Back at work, the staff had come to know Bonita and Carmen very well. They did not know Mrs. Wash, but understood that she was negative power for their team. She was not wanted. Jaza and Lloyd discussed the situation with Bonita and Carmen and began to pray with Wisdom Well team prayer participants at lunch. Bonita separated herself from everyone. Some days, Carmen and Bonita were together. They thought being together would create the force needed

35

to defeat Mrs. Wash. They both talked about the need to continue to care for the residents with tender loving care because caring was the only peace and positive power they had on their side.

It took everything Bonita had to pass medication that day and the dining hall was the last area. Mrs. Castile stood at the dining table, complaining for what could have been fifteen minutes. "The coffee is not right, where is my husband, the room is not clean the way I like it, where is my husband again, someone stole my teeth bowl, and where is my husband." She always thought her husband was cheating. She did catch him coming out of Mrs. Lee's room once. Needless to say, he was guilty and that was not a pretty sight. She knew that he was a cheater and she didn't trust the nurses, either. He cheated on her all of her married life and from what Bonita heard, she has made the world pay for his infidelity. From what the nurses all saw when he was undressed, they were all trying to understand why is Mrs. Castile was so upset. Bonita smiled after finishing the dining room meds and prepared to respond to Mrs. Castile when Mrs. Wash approached her from behind.

"Bonita, can you not control your patients?"

Bonita stood speechless. They were standing in the dining room with her patients looking on as Mrs. Wash proceeded to talk to her condescendingly. Bonita stood there, humiliated. Everything within her looked was tense as she glared at Mrs. Wash.

BITCH, she thought. The look on Bonita's face could not hide her feelings inside and she saw how stunned Mrs. Wash looked.

Mrs. Wash turned to Mrs. Castile and asked, "How can I make your morning better?"

"You are the one sleeping with my husband," she replied. "I knew it was you."

Mrs. Castile continued to accuse Mrs. Wash, growing louder as she talked. The staff and patients nearby laughed. No one thought to tell her that she suffered with dementia and she followed the nurses around the dining hall during medication pass often. Bonita smirked and Mrs. Wash scowled at her. It was obvious to Bonita that the two had entered into mutual warfare.

Lloyd came around daily, as well, but only to encourage Bonita. *This must be what God has for me to hear*, Bonita figured. His words were the separation of hate between Mrs. Wash and herself. With each day, Bonita found that her heart was becoming softer towards Mrs. Wash and she was not able to be as angry towards her. Love was found in every word Lloyd spoke.

During the day of the incident, lunch did not come fast enough and when it was lunchtime, her three friends ate at the same time. Bonita figured it must have been because of a guardian angel because this did not occur regularly.

Together, the team decided not to sit through this and continue to walk in misery and despair. They needed distraction from all of this madness. Bonita and Kate desired to stay in the Cast Iron skillet mode. Jaza frequented the Skillet often and shared all of the sports clubs secrets.

"Sooo," Jaza said, as she leaned back in her chair. "You're interested in talking to guys at the Skillet. So glad you're coming out. I like the new you."

"I exchanged my escape from the Wisdom Well to the Skillet," Bonita said. "The well is not an escape anymore. It has become a great place for misery. If I had a man, I would have an escape from life and this place. I'll settle for a piece of human distraction for now. My great escape will be the Skillet and its contents."

"Wake her up. Slap her face. Girl, that's you in there?" Kate chuckled. "And how are you?" Kate asked Carmen as she walked up.

"Not as bad as my friend. That woman is so awful, the patients are complaining. Mr. Jack had his daughter write a letter saying that she witnessed Mrs. Wash pointing her finger in Bonita's face, screaming threats."

"I don't believe she has that authority. She doesn't work here, she is merely orientating. I can't believe Mrs. Stanzer is going for that. Have you mentioned any of this to her, Bonita? Jaza asked, angrily.

Bonita lowered her head. "I am awfully embarrassed. I didn't think anyone saw that. The witch came to slam charts on the desk and threaten my job."

"Threaten your job in front of patients? She doesn't have that authority. She is in orientation. Bonita, why are you letting her do this to you? This weakness is not a part of your personality. Stand up for yourself; don't let her get away with this. You would not allow me to not defend myself."

"She said she has written enough on me that the day she is made my superior, I won't have a job. Carmen and I are devising a strategy and if that doesn't work, I figure I'll meet men and screw for my rent until I get enough nerve to tell my mom I'm broke and need to come home. Don't believe that, ya'll."

"No, that won't go down like that. You brought me up from a much worst place, just me and you," Kate said, beginning to sob. "I can't see you lettin' it go down like that."

Jaza sat at the lunch table with tears falling from her eyes, as well. And Carmen gazed toward Bonita whimpering, "Don't!" The three cried out for her to make it all go away. Bonita developed butterflies in her stomach, along with nausea and dizziness. She feared for these three young ladies' lives and developed the strength to fight. Kate could not revisit that place in life ever again; she would die. And all of the confidence that Jaza developed came from the encouragement Bonita gave her. All Bonita knew was to pray, though she believed God had left them alone and a man in her life at this time would be what she really needed. The girls committed to stay at one another's side, no matter the outcome. They would battle for another if she was not able to fight on her own. Bonita spoke to the girls with strength, vowing that nothing but life shall come from their unit.

"Kate, do you think DJ Rock It really likes me?" Bonita asked.

"I'm glad we have a more lively conversation. I don't know if it was your moves on the dance floor or his ESP, but he did leave the DJ booth for, was it twenty minutes? I have never seen him do that before. Do you like him like that?"

"Bonita, I'm glad we are on a better subject. I can't take it when your pretending not to be a winner," Jaza said, and the three girls laughed. "It is better to meet someone on the Internet. You get to talk to him and get to know him before he is in your face. This guy may not be your type. What about your Internet guy?"

"I don't know what you're talking about. I don't have an Internet guy, but can I express my true feelings without being judged?"

All three said, "Sure."

"Truly, it has nothing to do with this job, but I think I want to a man in my life."

The room was suddenly filled with shock. Although Jaza knew Bonita more intimately than the other girls, she sat with her mouth open.

Carmen struggled to move her mouth. "Ok then, I don't think we ought to start with the DJ."

"Why not? He's cute. He really came after her that night," Kate said. "I was there."

Carmen said, "The best thing to do is to go and observe him for a while without him knowing. Let's see what we see."

"It is not a club. We're going to the Cast Iron Skillet. It's a sports bar. Patrons come in to watch TV and socialize. Families go there, too," Jaza said.

"Why does it need a DJ?" Carmen questioned. "It's must be a smaller version of a club."

"Club or not, I'm going. We will have to define club or not later. I will be the black dress woman," Bonita said, laughing.

"Bonita, let's go early to spy on the great DJ Marl."

"Total agreement, Carmen. Let's get there early."

The ladies scattered to their assigned units to get the work done and to get out. Bonita and Kate rushed through their work. It was important to get off on time.

After work, Bonita called DJ Marl. He sounded happy to hear from her and he gave her instructions to wear red, as that night was Red Night. She politely informed him that she would not wear his brand, but confirmed her presence for the night. Kate asked her why she would not wear red and what brand had to do with it. Bonita could not believe that did not know what she meant. She explained that branding was meant in the same way that owners marked their cows.

"I wear red, he wears red and all the men in the place know to keep their hands off because I belong to the DJ. It won't happen."

❧

The night was popping off when Carmen and Jaza walked in the Cast Iron Skillet. The televisions were all on the playoffs. The place was full of people of both sexes and all ages, cheering for their teams. Paraphernalia from both teams covered the place and the atmosphere was charged. Both ladies ordered apple martinis, which was convenient, since martinis were half price on Wednesday nights.

"What time does the DJ start?" Carmen asked.

"Not until 10:00 pm. He is sitting at the bar, third seat from the left," Jaza said. He sat watching the game alone.

At 10:00 sharp, he took his throne in the DJ booth and the red dresses poured in. When Bonita walked in with Kate at 10:10, he immediately announced her.

"Diane, you're beautiful. Put on your red dress and high heels, lady. We gonna jam tonight."

The waiter brought over a green apple martini for Bonita. She instructed him to not bring any drinks if he doesn't have one for all four ladies at the table. He returned with four of them. The martinis flowed all night long. The girls laughed louder after each one.

"Well, if I don't get a date, I will surely sleep well," Bonita stuttered.

Jaza sternly replied, "I'm telling you, nowadays, this is not the way to meet a man."

Carmen laughed hysterically. "Jaza, you are drinking the drinks he is sending you."

"I didn't say nothing about him buying us drinks was bad."

"The English language goes down the toilet when you all drink. I am not missing one fine guy up in this place," Bonita said.

"Kate, are you discussing marriage? Is my language better?" Jaza said. The girls could not stop giggling.

"There are fine ass men in this place," Bonita said, looking around. "Check those jeans out, look at that ass! A girl can get chest pain for real in here. I'm going to dance with him and inconspicuously rub his ass. I've gotta –"

"Wait a minute," Jaza said. "Aren't we drinking drinks that you have another man buying for us? Bonita, who are you really? The surprise is what's inside!"

Bonita replied, "No, the surprise is in the martinis. Take care of me, girls, I am not responsible."

"Gee! Look at those black slacks, a man with a silver and black shirt. My panties are wet," Carmen said.

"Really, Carmen, I hope he is not gay," Bonita said, sarcastically.

"Give me another drink so that I can get some nerve to approach that stallion," Carmen said, drooling.

Jaza turned her head to see Bonita leave the table for the dance floor. "Have you seen him in here?" she asked Kate.

"He don't hang in here," Kate said. "How did she get Mr. GQ to meet her on the dance floor?"

"Oh, she didn't! She grabbed his ass!" Carmen said, laughing falling out of her seat. "No, she didn't apologize. My girl's got game. I'm almost finished with this drink and I'm going after the black and silver man."

"Ooh, the great DJ Marl is pissed," Kate said, giggling. "Don't sober up, girls because we ain't gettin' no more free drinks."

"Bump!! Not surprised, the DJ is clearing the dance floor. How is it that your old butt got Mr. GQ who none of us have seen before?" Jaza asked Bonita, who returned.

"I have got to keep the drinks coming because you young girls are not shakin' nothing. I am having so much fun. Lord, forgive me, please."

Bonita put her head down when the DJ announced the Lady in Red contest.

"The winner didn't wear red tonight," he announced.

Everyone at the table and the DJ looked toward Bonita. The dance floor was filled with ladies dressed in red.

"He's the Right Kinda Lover" began blasting and Bonita went to the dance floor.

"I may not be in the contest," she said. "But this alcohol has got me moving. I'm going to dance over the dance floor like a prima ballerina doing her solo."

Simultaneously, the girls called out, "Okay."

"The finest woman in the club, Diane," the DJ announced.

"Why does he keep calling her Diane?" Carmen asked.

"Contest fixed," the girls said.

When Bonita got back to the table, he had a note sent her asking her to wait for him to get off at 2 a.m. She wrote back that she had to leave to prepare for work tomorrow. He sent her back a telephone number with instructions to call more often. The girls decided that lunch tomorrow would be a conversation with Marlon..

᠎᠎᠎᠎᠎᠎᠎᠎᠎᠎᠎᠎᠎᠎᠎᠎᠎᠎᠎᠎᠎᠎᠎ ᥬᥬ

The next day for lunch, the girls all gathered around while Bonita dialed from Judy's cell phone.

"Hello?" the sexiest baritone voice answered.

"Hi, how are you?"

"Fine, who is this?" he asked.

"Sooo, do you give your phone number to everyone?" Bonita said, coyly.

"Diane." Marlon chuckled. "The caller ID showed Trinity Ministries. I started not to answer. What is Trinity Ministries?"

"I called from my Pastor's phone. I am a minister."

"A minister?" Marl laughed. "Not the way you put away the green apple martinis and danced all night with the owner of the place."

"Does that mean I can't love Jesus? I love the Lord with my whole heart, soul and mind. Who Is the owner?"

"Sorry, I meant no offense. That's just not the way I remember my Sunday school teacher, Let me get off of that touchy subject. The owner is the guy whose behind you were holding last night."

Bonita and the girls snickered softly.

"What do you do during the day?" he asked.

"Be about my father's business for real. I usually rest during the day and work at ten. I was hoping we could have lunch or early dinner so that we can get to know one another."

"That would be great if you are not in a relationship. I don't like drama and I don't want to cause any disturbances. But, I must let you know that I am not looking for anything serious at this time and it doesn't look like you are."

"I don't have any life drama. You are a nice lady and I would like to get to know you. Who knows what may happen. I am past the game stage and may be looking for someone to settle down with. So, can I pick you up for dinner?"

"No baby mamas, sleeping with the enemy girlfriends, stalkers or child support?"

The girls around Bonita all signaled in animation, but remained quiet as they waited for his response.

"No, none of that."

"You don't have kid? How old are you? That's unusual."

"I didn't say I don't have children. I have two kids."

"This is as hard as pulling teeth. You have two children and no child support? How old are you."

"It would be nice if we could talk about this over dinner face to face.

"I would prefer meeting you rather than you picking me up."

"Ok, but I am not a stalker. Do you like seafood?" he asked

"It's the best."

"6 p.m. at the Seafood Baron."

"Great, but how about 7:00 pm?"

"I guess I will have to see you then."

He hung up without saying goodbye. The committee had to discuss that and the girls' imaginations went wild.

"Must have had a woman walk in'."

"Jaza, you're stuck on Internet dating. Is that the motivation for your answer?" Bonita asked.

"Maybe he thought the conversation was over?" Carmen said.

Kate shook her head. "What planet is he from to think that he doesn't need to say goodbye. I feel it in my bones; somethin' is wrong. Alpine would sound like a much better date."

"Who is Alpine?" Bonita asked.

"Alpine is the Internet guy that Jaza met pretending she was Bonita," Carmen said. "She is persistent in believing that he will be her husband. Can you believe that?" And you won't consider meeting him? Jaza has experience on the Internet and she loves you. I am sure she would have screened him thoroughly by now. You don't have to be alone with Alpine."

"Oh no, what kind of mess is this?"

As Lloyd had walked up and joined their conversation.

Jaza asked, "Lloyd, what should we think of a guy who makes a first date and hangs up without saying goodbye?"

"Did he really hang up in your face? If he did, that would be disrespectful."

"Whether he did or did not intentionally hang up is debatable," Jaza answered.

"We will give him the benefit of the doubt. Who is he?" Lloyd asked.

"The DJ, DJ Marl," Bonita said.

"You girls clubbing? I didn't think that was your style. Don't go for the DJ. All of the girls have gone there."

"Uh huh," Jaza said, looking over at Bonita.

Lloyd glanced over at the Bonita. Feeling compelled to reply, she said, "It is not a club, it is a sports bar."

"What's the difference?" Lloyd asked, looking over his glasses. "You will have to sit down and teach me that one day. While I have you girls all here, I will give you all the invites to my brunch. I will be looking for all of you there."

"What's the theme? Would you like us to bring something?" Bonita asked.

"No, baby, this is a New Orleans throw down. Come on time. The theme this quarter is "The Essential Right Mind." Our menu this season is better than ever. My wife is putting on the Ritz. She is pouring on her event planner skills. She gets better at it with each event. Keep that on your mind as you prepare your hearts. Ya'll going to love it. We are excited to have ya'll coming."

Lloyd walked off to his unit, while the girls looked from one to another.

"Ok then!"

"Who told him we were all going to the brunch?" Jaza asked.

"I did not tell him we were all going to be there, he told us we were all going to the brunch and he seems excited about it," Bonita said.

The Seafood Baron. His DJ job must pay well. I'm ordering lobster and lamb chop, Bonita thought to herself as she met Marl who was waiting for her at the door.

"Hello, beautiful lady. You look absolutely stunning."

"Thank you. I don't feel like that. My job works me so hard. I feel tired. You don't see the black bags under my eyes, do you?"

He gently touched her face and said, "No, all I see is the sparkle in your eyes."

Bonita thought he didn't have to say the words exactly from the song. He ordered them both a green apple martini.

"Working so hard, you must be hungry. Would you like an appetizer?"

"I am going in for the main coursel. I'll have lobster and lamb chops. A Caesar salad would be nice."

Bonita saw his eyes stretch a little, but she didn't change her menu choice.. The meal ended up being great and the company was better. From the corner of her eye, she saw the shadow of a woman standing over Marlon, swinging her arms. The dessert menu went to the floor and she went out of the door. She didn't want to be stuck with that bill. Bonita met the valet driving her car around and once she got in, she laughed all the way home.

Bonita phone Kate when she arrived home,"Hello Kate? Wake up! Girl, you will not believe what has happened."

Kate laughed throughout the story. "Don't tell Jaza," she said. "She will swear more by the Internet."

"I don't think he had the money to pay the bill. He was dropping hints about the check," Bonita said. "I ignored everyone. His girl has that one."

"I wonder where some guys get the gall. You didn't stay around to see who she was and what she is to him. I woulda wanted to know."

"I won't be going to the Cast Iron Skillet for a while."

"I'm sure you won't let him stop you, killer. Besides, you don't know what happened."

"Do you realize that next weekend is the brunch and the fantasy party? We won't be able to do both."

"I like the way you change the subject when you don't wanna talk about something .But, yeah, the fantasy party is Friday night and the Brunch is Saturday for 10:00 am. We can do both."

"You girls are trying to die and go to hell and take me with you," Bonita said, with a sigh.

Chapter 5

"BONITA, WHY ARE YOU all dressed up? That's not... Where are your jeans?" Jaza asked.

"What! What's wrong with my clothing?"

"You don't dress up to go to the fantasy party. Wear your tight jeans and a sexy blouse."

"What is this fantasy about?" Bonita asked Jaza.

"What do you mean what is the fantasy about? I am here to pick you up. You should be ready. We will be late."

"Jaza, both of us can not fit in this closet."

"Well, get out so I can find you something appropriate to wear. Here, put on this outfit. It's cute. And while you're getting dressed, I'll call the girls to let them know we are on our way."

"Ok, how do I look? Stop pulling my clothes."

"You look nice, but it would have looked better with the blouse I chose. Let's go, we are going to be late."

"Jaza, what is this fantasy party about?"

Bonita thought she would get the details while she had her pinned down in the car. She thought it would be like acting out a skit or play.

A drama of some kind. She figured maybe they would all sit together, talking about their personal fantasies.

"It is a party that sells toys so that you can fulfill all of your personal fantasy and bring your personal fantasies up three or four notches," Jaza explained.

"God knows my fantasies need enhancing and uplifting."

"Like what? You want to move better when you're with your man, right?"

"What do you mean, move better?"

"Like when you're having sex, Bonita. You know moving, moving your hips…"

"You supposed to move? What are you talking about?"

"Huh?"

"What?"

"Bonita, have you ever had sex?"

"Stop it, yes!"

"Here we are."

"It's not a hall. It's at someone's house!"

"Durgesa, the party hound. She knows how to throw a party. And besides, with all of the toys, the girls would not feel free in a public place."

"What are we going to do with toys?"

They walked to the front door and Bonita spotted Carmen and Kate.

"Let's wait for them. Hey, you guys," Jaza called out.

"Something wrong, Jaza?" Carmen asked.

"Girl, I don't think Bonita has a clue of what tonight is about," she said.

"That's ok, Bonita. Stick by me. I'll show you stuff," Carmen said, reassuringly.

Durgesa opened the door with a wide smile.

"Hey ladies, come on in. I have had a couple of drinks, so get on my level!"

She handed Bonita a drink and said, "Here, suck a dick."

"A penis for a straw?"

"Girl, I can't drink that," Bonita said, blushing.

"It's just a plastic straw. It is ok, go ahead," Durgesa urged.

Kate reached over and pulled the straw from her cup.

"Thanks because I was not going to put my mouth on that," Bonita said.

"Be quiet," Jaza said, leaning over. "You are drawing attention."

"My," Dugersa said. "You a little stuck up."

Kate answered before Bonita could. "No, she is not stuck up. She don't know about all this stuff, that's all."

"Ready everyone? As we drink our orgasms, let's have a little fun with Ms. Kitty!"

Bonita watched as everyone started laughing. Kate made her a drink.

"Drink this vodka, Bonita. You're going to need it to have fun."

Jaza walked up and touched everything on Ms. Kitty's table.

"Ladies, we are starting off with lotions and potions," Durgesa said, as Ms. Kitty handed her a Q-tip with clit cream on it.

She turned her back, put her hand under her dress and it brought her down to her knees. Everyone wanted to try it. A strange lady asked for pheromones. Kate said she wanted to try the flavored oral stimulation gel.

Bonita thought to herself that this was too much and she wouldn't know what to do with this stuff. She'd been wanting a husband too long to settle for taking this stuff home alone.

"Carmen, why are you looking at the lubes and anal cream? You like it freaky, huh?" a girl laughed.

After a few drinks, Durgesa stood up and began giving instructions.

"We gon' play a few games, ladies. It is a little stiff in here. Let's form teams. Make two lines facing one another. The first team in and out of the panties wins. She distributed the panties red team and black team. When everyone was settled and ready, she blew on the penis whistle and the game began. Everyone laughed and fell over one another, stumbling. Bonita wasn't sure if either team even completed the game.

Kate prepared Bonita's drinks, while the other girls drank sex on the beaches and climaxes. Bonita was sure that she didn't want sex in her mouth.

The next game was called banana split. Everyone was loud and out of control. This game seemed to be the best part of the party. Everyone knew the game and was sad when it was over.

After that game was over, Ms. Kitty reset the table. Bonita heard Carmen singing, "Best part of the party, bullets and dildos of all sizes, sho' nuff climax time."

The stranger that stood next to Bonita in the panty contest screamed out, "Yep, multiple climaxes!"

Feeling light and free, Bonita yelled, "What is a climax?!"

"You fa real, chick?" Durgesa asked.

Bonita suddenly felt dumb and the entire room fell quiet. She was ashamed and she turned off her ears, but she could see Kate's mouth moving and she was sure that she was defending her.

The penises on the table were mind blowing. She looked around, trying to bring up another subject. There were big ones, tall ones, skinny ones and fat ones. Ms. Kitty held the small one that she called a bullet. There was a vibrating tongue and one that was called the Clitorific Plus and that was the one that Jaza had to have. Carmen liked the biggest dildo on the table; she got energized just holding it.

Bonita tried to smile and block out the times her husband would throw her down, rip her clothes from her body and force his penis into her vagina. She could not relate to the pleasure that the girls were excited about.

Ms. Kitty told them to take their favorite item and test how strong the vibration was. Bonita sat there, wanting the joy that the girls had when Durgesa came from nowhere and put a vibrator that was on between her legs next to her vagina. She began moving about and she was scared, but it soon became pleasurable. Embarrassed because it felt so good, Bonita said, "Ooh! Stop!"

"Leave it there long enough and you will climax. Sex feels good," Durgesa said and they all laughed together.

She then held Bonita down and put the vibrating tongue to her breast. She was stimulated from head to toe and my vagina felt electrified. But, Ms. Kitty became upset and told the girls they had to purchase those Items because they could not touch personal body parts. They moved Bonita into the sex swing that was hanging from the door, but Bonita made it clear that she didn't like it, so they took her down. The swing and the S and M toys were like sin and pornography, past fun. Bonita sat there thinking how she could order a dildo and vibrating tongue to take home without anyone knowing. But, it would not be good to have her first experience with feel good sex alone. She thought that she would rather have a man that she could make feel good, too. She felt different about sex and she wondered if she could let her curiosity wait until she got her man?

Help me, Lord!

They had a few more drinks and danced while Ms. Kitty went into the bedroom to take orders privately.

"It will be good to have a male stripper at the next fantasy party," Durgesa said. "What are we going to do next month? I'm glad Bonita let her hair down."

"We had a great time without judging ," Kate said. "The night was wonderful and drama free."

"I have found a new sister and bonding time is just what I needed," Bonita said, contentedly.

All the girls were in unanimous agreement. They all said their goodnights and went home relishing the moment and waiting for the next month.

∽

Driving home with Jaza was crazy fun for Bonita.

"Bonita, we are all different, yet one in the same. We all want to love, be loved and have a good time," Jaza said.

"The party was not what I thought. I had become skeptical, but now I am glad I didn't change my mind."

"The bag on the back seat behind you is a present from Durgesa and me."

"What!" She opened the bag and laughed. "Oh, you girls did not buy me this dildo and vibrating tongue!"

"We had to pay for it, anyway. And I already have a dildo. Bonita, I don't know how you got to the age you are without climaxing, but you don't need to get any older without it. You don't have to tell me, just do it for you."

"We have to go to the prayer brunch this morning. I would not live with myself if I didn't."

"None of us would be able to go to work Monday if we don't."

"Good night, rather good morning."

"Good morning, Bonita. I am so glad you came."

"I'm glad that I learned sex can be pleasurable. See you in a couple of hours."

Chapter 6

OH LORD, PLEASE FORGIVE me for the entertainment last night. Though I thought it to be unhealthy for my growth last night, the truth is that I enjoyed every minute of it. I imagined myself taking home and using some of the instruments that are called toys. Please don't let any little children find them.

Bonita felt uncomfortable going to the prayer breakfast. The conversation and party last night was not of the John 3:16 variety.

What am I turning into? Is this sin? Lord, am I compromising? If so, I am sorry. This is the first time in my life I am having fun. Is this really the true me? Must be from my daddy's side, Bonita thought. *Yes, I am discovering the true me. I will repent later if it is necessary.*

Her friends saved Bonita a seat at their table. Jaza signaled her over when she saw her walk in the door.

"Good morning in your church suit," Jaza said.

"Why did you dress like that?" Kate said, "This is a brunch."

Bonita looked around the room and saw that most of the ladies and men were dressed casually and the atmosphere was jubilant.

"I thought about prayer breakfast at church. Who are those guys at the table in the corner?"

"They are Lloyd's friends from New Orleans. They come to his brunch every time," Jaza said.

"Gee whiz, that is the finest group of men I have ever seen in my life. Why did I have to come in contact with them at prayer?"

"It is not like you would have done anything with them if you had met them somewhere else," Kate said.

"One day soon, and it won't be long, you girls won't say that and it will be true."

"Some ways are born in you and you will never change from that. It is not bad to be that way, Bonita," Kate said. "Carmen, do you know what you are talking about? Damn, what are they feeding those men down in Louisiana?"

"Kate, aren't you are thinking about marrying Mike Jike? And we are at prayer, so don't say those words. But, I have heard that the best food in the world is served in their parts of the country," Jaza said.

"Cook me some of that," Kate said. She spotted Sigrid at a table across the room. "I am glad Sigrid didn't sit at our table; we would not have been able to have fun."

"Sigrid is cool, she is my girl," Bonita said.

"You are the only one tight with Sigrid, Bonita. She likes to lecture so much," Carmen said.

"Lecture?"

"Yes, in our business trying to tell us what to do on our shift. She works nights," Jaza added.

"Sounds like she looks out for the patient. You guys don't become angry when I tell you what ..."

"You are on our shift and an RN –"

"Good morning, my friends," Lloyd said suddenly. "Stephanie and I are excited to have you in our home today to break bread and share the broke bread who is Jesus Christ. He is the nourishment for life and the answer to every need. Today, we will be focused on life. They say a mind is a terrible thing to waste, if we don't take control of our minds we lose our life.

"This brother going deep," Bonita whispered.

Kate turned to answer and Jaza turned and shushed them.

"This is the only church I get, three times a year," she whispered. The girls smiled and turned to listen.

"Your mind and your spiritual heart are one in the same. Your mind is the eye to your soul. I hope everyone has something to drink. Mingle and meet someone new before the next course. The Word says God judges a man by his heart.

"Jesus, he have to go all the way there. I feel guilty," Bonita whispered.

"Guilty for what, Bonita? You haven't done nothing. Nothin' happened. You are at brunch," Kate said.

"Kate, last night and this is real. The Holy Spirit brings conviction."

"Have mercy on her Lord, for she has sinned," Kate said, laughing with Carmen.

"Bonita, I think there is more to you and church than you're letting us know," Jaza said.

"You are very serious today. There's a definite change in your attitude, Jaza."

"I bet you could teach us the gospel," Jaza said.

"Why do you say that, Jaza?" Bonita asked. She was now aware that her past was being revealed to her friends. She tried to change the subject and her actions to deter their attention from her.

"Bonita," Kate said, with a distinct voice, "I have learned more from you about the Bible than any other person in my lifetime."

"I am so glad you did, but I am going to talk to the New Orleans men for a moment."

"I can't be..." Carmen murmured.

"Hello," Bonita said to the gentlemen. "I was compelled to walk over here to greet you as we were encouraged by the host. Are you guys professional sports players?"

The five gentlemen all laughed. One guy from the group asked, "Why do you ask that?"

"I see more lean meat over here that I have seen at the butcher shop. I couldn't stand it anymore and I came over to see if it was all real."

Guy number one blushed while guy number two answered, "No, I just like to stay in shape."

Guy number three stood and said, "I am a stripper."

The table went up in laughter and Jaza spoke loudly from behind Bonita, "No, that is not nice. Are you proud of that?"

The man sat down and looked on as Bonita said, "No, it's ok. Let's talk."

The other men looked at one another and Bonita embarrassed.

"Well, it was wonderful meeting you guys."

Bonita walked over to greet Sigrid.

"Hi, good morning," Sigrid said, giving her a hug.

"Good morning, Sigrid," Bonita said. "How are you enjoying the breakfast?"

"Convicted, but it is great. So is the scenery and the atmosphere."

Sigrid nodded her head towards the gentleman's table. "Always a great attraction. We older ladies like looking, also."

"Very nice."

Both ladies giggled.

"They are Lloyd's frat brothers. He introduced me as his mom away from home."

"Frat Brothers?"

"Omega Psi Phi fraternity. They were on line together."

"On line like a computer and they are fine, too."

Sigrid rolled her eyes.

"Bonita, you should never allow me to know more about the computer than you. No, in college when they were pledging the fraternity."

"Yes, I understand. I've heard you can't get closer than that. I wonder if the whole line is that fine."

"I think you've got that one right," Sigrid said.

All of the ladies at the table giggled.

"I should get my seat before the next phase starts," Bonita said.

"Jaza, are you CBing at the brunch," Bonita said, with her mouth turned down.

"That was not nice and at the prayer brunch… the nerve of him," Jaza said.

"How did you get behind me? He was teasing, anyway," Bonita said.

"Well, how do you know all of the stuff to say?"

"What stuff? And that was embarrassing, you screaming across the –"

"I'm sorry for embarrassing you," Jaza said.

"Ok, everyone. I hope you have met someone you did not know and enjoyed the hor d'oeuvres. While the main portion and desserts are being prepared for you, I will go forth with the word.

"We were talking about the mind and the heart. That which we have set our minds toward is the direction in which we develop our lives. In order to redirect our lives toward the organic word, we must redevelop our thinking. We have to be determined to not go through the same mess and come out depressed. Again, we do not have to become the products of our past history. We must be renewed in the spirit of our minds. That means we must change the way we see and think about each individual area of our lives. We are more than conquerors through Christ Jesus. That means we have the strength in us to make it all happen – all of our dreams and God's plan for us. Don't waste your thoughts. There are new opportunities and new destinies in our new minds.

"Get determined to not waste another moment. Set your mind on the pure word, see the Lord and you will become like Him. Then, no matter what comes your way, it will work out for your own good. God has given us a lot that we wait on Him for. You've got it. Set your mind on the promises of God, change your attitude first with yourself, discipline yourself and your emotions, prioritize and focus. If you get this into your mind and your heart, be prepared to win your promised destiny."

After the word, it took a long moment for anyone to move toward the food. Bonita was one of the last people to eat. She reviewed her life from twelve years old through this moment and she prayed about developing a new decision-making process. But, first she knew she had to develop a new wisdom on how I think. Bonita was in a deep thought process when she heard Kate calling her name.

"Bonita, Bonita!"

"I'm sorry, what?"

"Are you gonna eat? We are the last ones in line to fix our food," Kate said.

"Yes, let's eat. When I leave here, I'll have a lot to think about. I hope this is preparing me to go back to the foolishness of our job. I have to prepare my mind in the Word for that place."

"How do we do that, Bonita?" Carmen said. "I was thinking the same thing."

"Let's eat and forget about it now," Bonita said. "This food is so good. What is this, crawfish, Monica?"

Chapter 7

"*I* BE FUCKED IF THIS low down dog thinks I'm gonna take her shit lying down this time. This bitch has got to be out of her mind! I will go to jail before I sit in a homeless shelter again, crying because she has got her nuts off on me! Not this round, whore. The mother is not getting her rocks off on me again. I am going to set this bitch on fire! That is one set I will not repeat on anybody's stage. My stage in life has to go up or I'm going out!"

Bonita was violently screaming and throwing her belongings around her apartment. *I don't give a shit!* The distress and despair had taken over. She knew she had lost it, but the rage had taken over her emotions and she was out of control of herself.

She jumped from the bed where she was throwing clothes across the bedroom and fell to her knees.

Lord, I don't guess it is appropriate for me to call on You this time. I want to throw up on myself right now! If I'm going to survive this, You had better show up for me now. Jesus, I am not making demands, but there is no way I am going to walk out of the nursing home tomorrow, having accepted my character torn down. The humiliation would be unbearable. Jesus, I have been too good to that place. I have cleaned more shit than – Oh, God, if You are real right now, you would be working on my heart. I don't feel like You, don't sound like You and I don't want to. How could You let this be? If You are God, stand up for me. I can't live through another stinking, alcoholic rapist tearing at my body because I have nowhere to sleep. I can't take another beating. I want to kill something! God! You promised that I had You. You promised I would not have to be alone. No way are You all powerful and I have to do this again. Don't let my heart be bitter!

Bonita could hear the phone ringing at the back of her misery. She knew it could only be Jaza. *I wish I had not answered that woman. The truth is, Lord, I could have punched her in the mouth. Thank You for Jaza. What gives her the audacity to stand in my face with the same lies and accusations that destroyed my last job and my reputation? Pull me together, Lord.*

The tedious ringing of the phone only intensified her inflamed attitude. Bonita snatched up the phone and angrily screamed, "Hello?!"

"Bonita, what's wrong."

It was not Jaza. She tried to calm herself so that she could decipher whose voice she was hearing.

"Bonita, are you ok?" the voice repeated. "What's wrong?"

"Mama?" she asked, regretting her anger. "Mama, I'm ok."

"Oh my baby, what is wrong? I had been thinking about you a lot today and your greeting caused me to feel emendated with fear. Oh heavens. What is going on? And don't tell me nothing, I can hear it in your voice and my heart feels jolted. Should I be out on the next plane?"

Jesus, calm me down. She cannot come to this town while I am in this place and this situation.

"Mom, it's nothing I can't handle. I'm ok."

"What –"

"Calm down, Mom. I love the sound of your voice. I have been a little stressed on my job. I am ok. I have it all under control. I have such a headache."

"I have not ever heard you get that upset. What is going on? What is happening to you?"

Sighing and holding back tears, Bonita spoke with a soft stressed voice, "Ma, I'm ok. Don't start worrying about me I can't handle that at this time. I'm ok."

"You have not been yourself for a while, Bonita. I cannot imagine what is happening, but I never thought I would live to see the day that you would lie to me. You are not the child that I raised. What has happened to you? Is it a man?"

"I wish it was as simple as a man, Mom."

"Did you get another bad husband, Bonita?"

I never told her about my horrible marital experience. I won't feed into that because I don't want to give her any information that would cause her to be in a worse panic. I just want to get off the phone so that I can cry myself to sleep.

"Mom, I will not get married without you being present. I love you very much, Mom. I'm going to make you proud that you are my mother. I will give you something to boast to Mrs. Adiy about, I promise you."

"Darling, you are my most prized possession. You are all that I have in life. Nothing is worth more than you to me. You are my life's trophy and I could not be more proud of anything else that I possess in life. I love you."

Bonita softly said, "Mom, I needed that more than you'll ever know. I'm so tired and I have to get up in the morning. Can I call you back tomorrow?"

"Ok, my daughter. You take care; you are all that I have in this world. If you don't call me back tomorrow, I will be on a plane tomorrow night."

"Ok mom, I love you."

Her mother allowed her to end the conversation, but Bonita knew that there was no way that her mother believed she was ok. Tears began to soak Bonita's pillow as the fear of repeating her downfall flooded her memory.

"Jesus," she cried, "I can't do this again and survive. I need Your help, Lord."

৶৹

Bonita woke up late and her eyes were swollen shut from crying through the night.

Three hours of sleep, how am I going to make it today? I wonder if I should have called out, she thought as she picked up the phone.

Bonita lay in bed until evening without any strength to fight the depression she was going through. Snot and tears were her breakfast and lunch. She did speak to her mom shortly, but she had not been able to mask her sadness. Suddenly, there was a loud bang at the door that sounded like a great thunderstorm. Bonita jumped up, startled.

"Open the door!" Jaza called out. "Open the door, now! Are you ok?"

"I am opening this door because if I don't, you won't go away," she said, as she pulled herself from bed and walked toward the front door. "Ok, ok!"

"I came right over when I heard you called in because that is something you don't do. You would not leave me like this. I can't leave you like this, either. What is wrong? You look horrible. Come on, let's get you cleaned up."

"Girl, give me a break."

Jaza held her nose. "Pew, your breath stinks. Mouth care first."

"Jaza, I don't have the energy. I can't do this."

"I understand, I have the energy for you. And besides, I can't leave you with breath like that.

Jaza walked Bonita into the bathroom. She prepared her toothbrush and toothpaste and started the mouth cleaning process. She drew a beautiful bubble bath that was the perfect temperature.

"This is the furthest you go. I can do the rest myself. I'll be ok," Bonita said. "You can go now if you'd like."

"No, I'm not leaving until you're up, smelling good, laughing and functioning. You have to be ready, Bonita."

"Ready for what?"

"Ready for your future. When it gets this bad, it can only get better."

Bonita cleaned herself up. When she was done with her bath and dressed, the two sat and talked about their dreams and fantasies for hours. Laughter was Bonita's medicine for the remainder of the night. She held onto Jaza so tightly. She was thankful because Jaza was a true friend and Bonita needed her in her life. She would have laid there for days had Jaza not gotten her up. The two renewed their covenant to love, protect and pray for one another, vowing to never allow anything to come between them.

Bonita woke the next morning with fear and determination battling for her heart. Trying to pray, she struggled to remember all that the Lord had brought her through. As she began to hear the laughter of last evening roaring through her mind, she held onto that moment of gladness in desperation to make it through the day. Somewhere inside of her mind and emotions, she felt the words, "Sometimes, God draws your enemies close to see you get blessed. They know what you've been through and know that only God could have lifted you this high." She looked in the mirror deep into her own eyes.

"This is my job, and I thank You for my Job. I don't claim it, I receive it. Thank You, Jesus. I am going to work tomorrow believing You have not left me."

"Bonita, I need you to be calm when I tell you this."

"Oh no! What now!"

"Ms. Stanzer came by this morning. Your name is not on the schedule to work for the next two weeks. Your assignment has been given the new LPN Mrs. Stanzer introduced yesterday."

"What are you saying, Jaza? What is this? What is going on? Why didn't you tell be about this last night? I needed to know this."

"Last night, all I could do was get you ready to live again. I couldn't tell you anything that I could not explain. That would have killed you. We can't afford for you to crash; we need you to make it through this, no matter what. We need you."

"What the hell is this, Jaza? Did I just get fired from this shit job? Have mercy! Unemployed again... I can't take losing everything, again. I've given this place nothing but the best. You know how much better this place is for the residence because of me and my hard work. Oh, Lord, I can't believe this."

"Calm down, Bonita, Calm down. We don't know what is going on. When she came out looking for you, she did not look unhappy or disturbed. I believe you shouldn't try to imagine what happen, but first hear her out. It is like you always say, 'The Lord is with us and He foresees every moment of our lives.' Let's see what this is about first. Calm down."

Bonita walked away swiftly as Jaza attempted to comfort her. She stood in the restroom mirror, crying and praying before stepping into Mrs. Stanzer's office.

"Why, Lord? Why me again? I can't handle this. Three times, she attempted to look in the mirror to clean up her face and three times, she burst into tears. Each time, she became angrier. She had decided that no one would ever rape her again, especially not this LPN job. *No way*, she decided.

Bonita tried to be humble and calm, but that was not how she presented herself. She stormed into Mrs. Stanzer's office.

"What is going on here, Mrs. Stanzer? I have worked so hard for you on this job. In spite of my position as a LPN, I performed as an RN with integrity and determination for the lives of these old people. You owe me nothing for that. But to call me in to terminate my job after all I've been through here is inhumane. Have you released me of my job? What —"

Mrs. Stanzer gently approached Bonita and said, "Have a seat, Bonita. I need you to calm down. I need to talk with you. I want to ask you what you are talking about, but I need you to calm down first."

"Calm down? I know what you are trying to do to me and you want me to calm down?"

"Yes, for that very reason, I need you to calm down. I wanted to meet you on your arrival this morning prior to anyone saying anything to you. I missed you coming in. I've been waiting for you."

Bonita stared at Mrs. Stanzer and felt a very strong dislike in her heart. She thought to herself, *Lord, get me out of her before I bash her face in.*

"I see you are upset, so I'll get right to the point."

Bonita took a deep breath and looked away from Mrs. Stanzer.

"Your hard work that you were not paid for or acknowledged for has been recognized. It would be good if I can share our dilemma with you."

"Yes, I will need you to share your dilemma with me. My heart and mind are racing in four directions right now."

"I will need you to keep this confidential. We have been operating without a Director of Nursing for months now because of our negative status with the state. We had to bring a lot of paperwork up to code that had been neglected and unattended by the past director. Without knowing that you came in and diligently worked, you saved this place and allowed all of us to have a job. Though we had many penalties to pay, our credentials have been restored without probation and limitations. We will be placed back on the Medicare and Medicaid payroll. We, the owner and I, thank you for signing the documents and standing in that office without compensation. Yes, we have been discussing you. Your work here has been remarkable. Your care for our residence is genuine and many family members have written us about you. We are so grateful to have you."

Bonita sat in awe. She could not believe what she was hearing. She thought about how she stressed for months. Mrs. Wash is still here. She must not have gotten to her yet. *How do I feel at this moment? God, what am I to do or say? How am I to act?"*

"Bonita? Bonita, have you heard anything I've said to you?"

"What? I'm sorry, what did you say? Yes, I did hear you. I will need clarification on what are you saying. Do I have a job?"

"'Do you have a job?' I did take for granted that you would accept the new position."

"What new position? You were talking, but you never said anything about a job for me. I am aware that I am not on the schedule. I do not have a station. Where am I going to work? I thank you for appreciating me. I did that work because I love people and I don't want to lose my skills as a RN. I need a job. Do you understand, Mrs. Stanzer? I need to work until I can find another job."

You can sit there looking dumb founded if you want, Bonita thought. *I feel like Set It Off right now. It is not going down and I walk out with nothing. Bring it on because I'm going to jail for something. I'm going to make it worth me having to tell Mom.*

"Bonita, we are hoping you would take the Director of Nursing position. There is no one better fit than you. We need you to say yes."

Bonita sat, speechless.

"What? Ahh! Oh my God? What does all of this mean?" She could feel herself hyperventilating and she tried to calm down.

Bonita and Mrs. Stanzer sat talking for almost an hour when a thought suddenly crossed Bonita's mind. *I'm going to be supervisor for my friends whom I have learned all of their ways and backstreets on the job. How can I do this?*

Bonita said to Mrs. Stanzer, "I now have to try to see my friends as my workers. I don't know if I can do that. Some of the things I know about of them they would have not told me if I were their boss. How can I be fair to them? Maybe this would not be a good idea. There is no way Mary Ann would continue doing the things she does. It is awful the way she handles the residence. If I hear Joey scream at Mr. Lever again, I will have to say something towards his inappropriate behavior. Lord, how do I handle this now? Part of me feels like I am betraying them. Why did you let me see all of this and then make me their boss? Oh God..." She then realized she had said too much to Mrs. Stanzer.

Mrs. Stanzer looked her in the eyes and said, "No one else could do what needs to be done like you can. We believe that you will save our workers' lives and save this place. We will all benefit, Bonita. Say yes!"

She waited a moment, then spoke again. "As I explained, our site review went well and our accreditation is coming up rapidly. We do need to prepare our charts for audits, infection control and manuals for updates. We need your help. Please accept the position. We can't offer the pay that you would deserve from wearing so many hats, but there will be an increase. Can we discuss that?"

Bonita ended up left the office ecstatic. She walked the halls, looking for Jaza. *God did sneak up and bless me,* she thought. Just as she turned the corner, she did run into Mrs. Wash.

"I'm sorry," Bonita said.

"Yes, you are a sorry human being. Why are you gallivanting in the hallways? Shouldn't you be on your unit?"

"My unit? Where would that be?"

Bonita felt confidence surging through her body. She could feel herself preparing to tell this woman everything she has thought of her. Except on the job, she would not be able to say some of the words she had thought in the past.

"So, did you think of a hallway for me yet?" Bonita asked, sarcastically.

Mrs. Wash looked surprised and confused for a moment.

"Girl, you have no gall or back bone. Where do you get off –" She stopped her sentence and said, "Let me put it another way. It would behoove you to go to your unit to continue cleaning old ladies' bottoms. That is, if you want a job. I see you have poor retention in that area."

"If I were you, I would be concerned about what you are saying. I do take pride in cleaning anyone's bottom who can't clean their own because I'm a real nurse. Nothing any patient needs is too much for me to take care of. And as far as the hallways are concerned, I give them out now. Be careful and close your mouth," Bonita said.

"How dare you disrespect me in that manner? I don't know what could have convinced you that you could possibly be one to give out assignments. I've worked with you; you don't have enough knowledge to convince me that you graduated from a university. You'll never make it and I'll see to that. Again!"

"It won't work this time," she retorted with a smile as Mrs. Wash's face began turning red. "What have I ever done to you to make you hate me this way? What is it that I have done to you? No one could hate another as much as you hate me. You don't know me, woman. What is wrong with you?"

"You mean, what is wrong with you. You have everything that was supposed to be mine, I hate..."

Bonita looked into the eyes of the woman who faced her and saw the eyes of the girl who tried to rip off her Calvin Klein jean outfit.

"Jean," she whispered.

"That's right, bitch, and if we were somewhere else, I would rip you apart."

"We are not children anymore. We won't be fighting in the street and we won't be killing one another."

"This is where I would punch you in your mouth. I had no childhood. You and your whoring mom took my dad and our welfare. You don't deserve what you have. I hate you."

Bonita stood there, startled for a moment before she was able to reply. "At least now, I can make some sense out of this madness. Mrs. Wash and Jean, one and the same."

Jean stepped up to Bonita, with anger and tears in her eyes. "I don't have nothing to stop me from taking you apart right here in this hallway."

"Yes you do. You may be a lot of things, but you would never make it in jail. And besides, your kids would have to live with me."

"Bitch, die! Die, bitch, die! I wish you would fall off the earth!" Her hand whipped out and slapped Bonita across the face.

A janitor suddenly stepped between the two ladies. He looked over to Bonita and said, "Are you ok, Miss Bonita?"

"Yes, Mr. Gaylord. I am ok."

Jean stormed away.

With her face stinging, Bonita sat in her office for hours, trying to decipher the matters of her life. Just as she moved forward, she got slapped back by Jean, her half-sister. *How had managed to find me after all this time? How could Dad leave us in this state? I had not given her a thought since she barged into my wedding, trying to destroy my day. And she wants me dead! Oh my dear Lord. I wish Alpine would be at home now. Talking to him would make it all better.*

After an hour and a half, Bonita walked the halls, but was unable to find Jaza. *She must be on one of her rendezvous out of the building. Lord, what am I going to do with all of this mess? Somehow, I think*

Mrs. Stanzer is counting on me to fix this place. She doesn't care what the cost.

She knew that Jaza frequently walked off the unit for at least three hours and often didn't take care of the patients properly. Bonita ran her hands through her hair, bewildered and wondered if she had bitten off more than she could chew? She knew in her heart that Jaza could never respect her as a boss. Thinking of it like that, would it be fair to her for Bonita to call her out on the many violations that she knew Jaza committed? Bonita didn't want to work with me on the same unit and she would have not tolerated her actions as a supervisor. But as a friend and equal co-worker, she realized that it was not her place to judge or correct her work ethics. She wondered if she would lose her friend. She wondered if she and Jean could ever be sisters. God only knew that she could use a sister. Screaming inside, she sat at her desk and cried for a long while and later, went home, trying not to think about the events that had occurred that day.

Bonita completed a stressful week as Director of Nursing at the Wisdom Well Nursing Home. She arrived early on the last day of the week to dump on Sigrid before shift change. As she approached, Sigrid opened her arms and wrapped them around Bonita's shoulders.

"I know, I could see it in your face all week. It's going to be alright. But, I want to say congratulations on your RN position."

"Sigrid, do you truly think that I am going to make it? I'm going to have to lose friendships. I would replace every employee if I had gone through it myself. And Jaza's my friend."

"What you have experienced is not related or relative to this experience. Jealousy raged in your past and tried to devour you because it tried to stop what you are doing at this time. It takes the courage that is already embedded in your soul for you to make it through. The powers that be have seen the influence you have over this staff. You can get these young people to do anything. You are being tried;

let them run into a stone wall. I do believe in you and you're going to make this a better place."

"Oh no, Sigrid. Jaza will not respect me if I discuss her –"

"Stop right there. What you and Jaza have runs deep inside of both of you. She will be embarrassed at herself for a moment. But, she knows that you care for her and will take your correction as an asset to her character before it is all over. I've been around for a minute and I know."

"What about Mary Ann and the rest of them? Mary Ann is a mess all by herself."

"When these young people realize that you're building them toward their own better future and that you will only be as good as they work, this place will be new. Mrs. Stanzer is a very smart woman for placing you in that position."

"Really, you think so? Why do you say that?"

"You should have seen this place and these people before you got here. They have really improved."

"Oh my God. Really?"

"Patients receive care now and the nurses work better to compete with you. Before you came, Jaza did more gallivanting and no work. Now, her patients are clean before she goes off. I always wondered where she went and what she was into. As for Mary Ann, she has not cursed at a single resident since you've been here. Each employee has shown improvement in caring for the residents. Now we are waiting for the master to put the icing on the cake."

"Have mercy, me too!"

"Bonita, that one flew over the coo coo's nest. I was speaking of you, darling."

Chapter 8

*T*HE WEEKEND CAME BEFORE Bonita knew it. This has been the toughest week in her life, now that she was charged with supervising her friends. Some of the things she knew about some of them made her feel weary. There is no way that Mary Ann could keep her job as she continued to abuse the residence. Bonita looked in the mirror and thought that abuse is a strong word. She told Joe that if she ever heard him scream at Mr. Lever again, he would be suspended.

Lord, how do I handle this? Am I am being extreme?

She had the weekend to rest and she knew she would need it. On Monday, she would begin to sit down with them individually. For the hard changes, she decided to position them to be the decision makers and to choose a leader from among themselves. She would leave the responsibility of making the difference on them. That was her plan of survival.

She had prayed for this RN job, but after one week, she felt stretched beyond sanity. Bonita looked in the mirror. *On Monday, I will get back on it, but tonight, I need a little Rose' Courvoisier to relax.* She took a few sips and fell back on the bed with her legs in the air. *Me, the boss. Wow.*

The phone suddenly rang and she reached over and picked it up.

"Hello, Bonita!"

"Hi, Jaza!"

"Are you drinking tonight? It's Friday and the drinks are on your girls. The Cast Iron Skillet is where we are taking you to celebrate. That's only because we don't know too many other places."

"Ok. What are you wearing?"

"Since this is a special occasion, we are all wearing dresses appropriate for the Skillet on Friday night, of course."

"And I'm dressing in black; I don't know who will be there."

"Glad you didn't give me a hard time. DJ Marl ill be there."

"Not that joker, please."

"I see you still don't understand the man's attraction. Why didn't you believe the man's story that that woman was just someone who misunderstood their friendship?" Jaza asked, laughing.

Bonita giggled and said, "Ok, girl, what time?"

"Be there for 8:30 and bring your celebration shoes with you."

The four women were in full blast on the dance floor after two green apple martinis. Just like Jaza said, DJ Marl was sending the drinks and was very mindful of Bonita.

When he got a moment, he came over to Bonita with a smile. "Would you like to dance?"

"Dance again? You won't get paid tonight, Substitute DJ Marl ."

"Auto pilot. I know what this crowd likes. Right now, I am trying to learn what it is that you like, besides green apple martinis."

"I got a promotion and a raise on my job. I like that."

"Ooh! Congratulations! I wish I had known. I would have bought you a gift."

"You would guess what I liked, right?" Bonita turned to face DJ Marl. "I won't be able to find a guy if you keep hanging on to me. By the way, what is the color for tonight?"

"Stop it, Bonita. Give me a chance."

"Maybe I'll think about it," Bonita said. *I can't be that desperate, can I?*

The group took to the floor during the line dance medley, laughing, dancing and having a great time. They drew the attention of the crowd on the dance floor. As the four left the floor, Kate asked, "You havin' a good time, Bonita?"

"Yes! I just need DJ Marl to stay out of my face for a minute. There are so many fine men in this place."

"Is that Sister Bonita talking?" Carmen asked.

"Are you thinking about getting a life? Planning to go home to more than a good book?" Kate added.

"I think I want a man of my own, like one forever."

The three of her friends stopped and their mouths opened wide and they looked around at one other.

"Okay. Well… I am trying to understand what you feel," Jaza said.

Carmen and Kate laughed uncontrollably.

"Loneliness can make you feel… Damn, is it the martini or the finest asses on the finest men up in here tonight?" Carmen wondered aloud.

"Carmen! Both of you ladies are out of the closet tonight," Jaza said. "You trying to take something to take home, too."

Kate became serious for a moment. "I understand the demon of loneliness. It can make ya do some things that'll never cross ya mind. Or be with guys that ya know mean ya no good. But, you would convince yourself that it is betta than being alone. Be careful, ladies. Ya both are special."

"Bonita, don't worry, I have someone for you. You will meet him tomorrow night," Jaza said.

"No, Jaza. If you have someone, I already know he is an Internet guy."

"They are the best. Bonita, give him a chance. It will be a double date, anyway. You will not be with him by yourself and this is a weekend of celebration."

"I think you should go Bonita," Carmen said. "Try him"

"Are serious about the date thing?" Jaza asked. "I don't believe you would be irresponsible in a relationship, especially if sex was involved. What do you have to lose?"

"I am not meeting a computer man. What do I have to lose? My life. He could kill us all. Do you know anything about him? Where does he work? Where does he live? What is his license plate number to give to the police?"

Kate rolled her eyes and said, "I say ya over the top, Sista."

"I have been talking to him for weeks, pretending I was you," Jaza said, with a grin.

"What am I going to do with you?"

Carmen interrupted. "Excuse me. Can you get me a man from the Internet?"

Just then, a man walked up to asked Carmen to dance and the party started all over again. By three a.m., the girls left, closing the place down for the night. Bonita had never been out that late partying before and neither had Carmen, who was too tired to drive, so they both jumped in Bonita's car and went to her apartment.

∞

"Is it 11:00 a.m. already?" Carmen moaned as she looked at her phone sleepily.

"I am in the restroom. Breakfast is ready," Bonita called back. "I have a toothbrush out for you in the bathroom. Meet me in the kitchen for a gourmet breakfast."

"How do you do this, Bonita? This looks so delicious."

"I am so happy to have someone to cook for and care after."

"Bonita, I so need someone to care for me. I am exhausted."

"From the job."

"No, I thank God for that job and passing my boards was the greatest gift that God has ever given to me," Carmen said.

"I see such stress in your head. The celebration last night was good. We had a great time. What's wrong?"

"It is a long story, Bonita. My grandfather brought me to America when I was fifteen years old. You do know that fifteen is a girl's big birthday in my country, right?"

"I did hear that."

"My papi thought I was the smartest girl and that I had the chance to breath. He gave me citizenship, brought me to America and educated me because he believed that I was smart enough to get my education and help bring the rest of the family over – these pancakes are good. But, before I could finish school, my papi died. Some of my relatives came over on grieving passes and others members of my family could not wait for citizenship, so they hitched their way here. Now, I am working to take care of all of them."

"How many are there?"

"In my house, there are nine of us, now."

"You will never be lonely," Bonita said, laughing. "Look at the bright side of things. You know they're ok."

"Not ok! Any day or any time, one of them can be stopped and deported. I am tired and afraid."

"You can always come here to get a break."

"I found someone to marry my brother off to, but her family found out and cancelled the wedding. Threatened to call the "people on us." So, that was the end of that."

"Your situation is one that lots of Americans don't understand and aren't sympathetic about."

"How about you, Bonita. How do you feel?"

"This breakfast discussion is not about me and what I think. I am here for you."

"That means you don't appreciate us being here. I am not mad; I want to understand how people can feel that way. What is the difference between flying in with papers and driving for days to America in a car? If I understood that way of thinking, I would not be bitter"

"You truly want me to discuss my feelings? Are you ready for that Carmen?"

"Ready or not, I live it daily. There is nothing that will change between us. But, all of this will be easier to live with if I had a greater understanding."

"Well, the law is partially there to control numbers. I am sure that everyone who applies to come to this country is not allowed. We would have no place for naturally born Americans."

"I can understand that. But, we all have a hard time, citizenship or not."

"I guess Americans are angry so they take it out –"

"Mad at what?"

"At everyone who is here illegally, working and making tax-free money and getting free health care. Tax-paying citizens are paying –"

"Bull. I pay taxes, check my –"

"You are not here illegally."

"I take care of my family," Carmen said. "I work and pay taxes. When the males go out, being hustled in legal homes, the pay is pennies on a dollar and we all pay taxes at the store with those two dollars they've made. There are corner doctors we have to trust and pay top cash dollar because we can't buy insurance or go to the hospital for fear of being turned in. My younger siblings didn't ask to come here, but they're here."

"Is that an excuse? Parents and children go –"

"I understand that, Bonita. What I am saying is that my brothers and sisters knew nothing of this country, nothing. Now that they are here, do you think that they would want to go back to the poverty? They have been here most of their lives; they would not know how to live in the old country."

"Thanks to the new law Obama passed, children in school can stay here until the schooling is complete. It may not seem fair, but as fate would have it, they are illegal. I don't agree with paying for their schooling. That is not my responsibility. You guys want us to change our country to little Mex..."

"Bonita, why?"

"You're mad if we don't speak Spanish, the cost of the services that you don't pay for is driven up because you want us to have interpreters. You're mad because you are put out of the school we are paying for and –"

"I hear what you are saying."

"I feel like this, Carmen. The wrong road could never become the right road. It can only be made right by doing the right thing, the right way."

"But if you listen –"

"During the wrong thing over a length of time does not make it right. It just make you wrong longer and you should be made to pay for your actions."

"Bonita, you don't mean that."

"We better stop talking about this before one of us becomes angry. Some of this is my own feelings and some of it is the feeling of others that I know."

"Ok, we don't have to talk about it anymore. This breakfast is good. Did you make these pancakes from scratch?"

"Bisquick. I did squeeze the oranges, though."

"What are you going to do with the rest of your day?"

"I am going to go on the date with the Internet guy tonight."

"Oh my heavens, no. I never thought I would see the day!"

"Do you think I'm desperate?"

"I think you are something. Internet dating sounded like it was a nightmare for you, the way Jaza said it."

"What the hell am I doing? I want to get on with my life. A little testosterone would help a little bit."

"Do not let him come here," Carmen warned.

"Oh, I will be driving my own car and it is a double date with Kate and Koffer."

"Oh Jesus, heaven has to be with you. Kate's history with Internet dating speaks for itself."

"I'm going to try it just this once."

"Well, I'll be home praying."

"I mean what I said, Carmen. You can spend the night anytime you'd like."

"Thank you, Bonita," Carmen said, as she hugged her.

After breakfast, they prepared to go get Carmen's car from where she left it the night before. Jaza came out and tagged along with them. On the way, the girls talked about the upcoming date and what Bonita should do and expect. As she got out of the car, Carmen told Bonita that the conversation they had today was for information only and that they never needed to speak of it again.

"What conversation was that?" Jaza asked.

Carmen replied, "Internet dating."

"You haven't influenced her negatively have you, Carmen?"

"Me? No, never, Jaza. I only want the best for her."

"Ok, girl, we will call you first thing tomorrow to let you in on the details," Jaza said, as Carmen got out of the car.

"Maybe Bonita can make breakfast again."

Jaza talked and tried to relieve Bonita's anxiety concerning her date with the Internet guy. Bonita decided that she would shop for a new outfit, but it could not be red, nor black because she would look too sexy.

"I am labeling this day as my new beginning," Bonita said.

"Bonita, I am so happy for you. With the job and this. I hope that tonight will prove to be special for you. I pray that he is your soul mate."

"I am looking to be found by my spirit mate. I want a man to know me by my spirit."

"Same difference."

"Far from the same, Jaza. A man can not satisfy your soul or flesh without knowing anything about you."

"I can get into conversation on a subject that I don't know anything about, but I do believe in love at first sight. I'll talk about the job. Bonita, are you going to come in bulldozing us?"

"Bulldozing. I hope bullying is nowhere in my personality. There will need to be some changes that must take place, but I do not intend on doing any changes without the participation of the staff. Most of the changes will come from you all, but any negative activity or mistreatment of the patients must stop or some folks won't have a job. As the boss, I cannot allow some of this stuff to go on."

"Well, Mary Ann is out of a job. That is horrible. Someone should have stopped her a long time ago."

"Jaza, I just got a job. I know what it's like to be out of a job with nothing to eat, to lose everything and ultimately be homeless."

"Look at it like this Bonita. Those people in the home could be your mother. You're in this position and harsh decisions sometimes come with the territory. If she or anyone else did such things to my parents..." Jaza looked at Bonita with passion in her eyes. Those residents and their families are paying for her to do such things to them."

"Why then, Jaza, do you truly think I should judge and respond so harshly?"

"You have a different kind of power now. You are our boss," Jaza retorted.

"Jaza, my friend, let me say this. If it had not been for you, I would not have made it through this. I think I would've died. You are my friend and nothing can stop that. I would expect because you are my friend, you would be the best nursing assistant on the floor. But, I must also say that I will not differentiate how I treat the staff."

"Bonita, I am on this job to support myself until I find a rich husband, someone to love and to take care of me for the rest of my life. I do not have intentions to stay on this job. As you say, this job is not what defines me. As soon as I get the right man to take care of me, I will be out of your hair."

"Hey Jaza, we are celebrating, remember? We will have a meeting another time to talk about this. Let's have fun, play and enjoy this weekend."

Jaza and Bonita walked through the mall, laughing, shopping and enjoying their day until the time of the date finally arrived. They headed out to meet the men.

Bonita knew which guy was her Internet date because he stood in the lobby with Koffer. Bonita walked up to the three of them and said, "Hi."

"Hello, you must be Bonita. I am Alpine. Surprisingly, you don't look anything like I imagined. You are beautiful."

Bonita looked puzzled and said, "Okay."

Jaza nervously stumbled over some words that made no sense, then blurted, "Uh, Bonita, I have to go to the restroom. Come with me."

"Darling, are you ok? Are you alright?" Koffer asked, worriedly.

Everyone looked around the table at one another.

"Oh, well. I don't know what to say!"

"Say about what, darling?" Koffer asked.

Jaza whispered to Koffer a little louder than she thought, "I had conversations with Alpine pretending to be Bonita. I chose him carefully and I am sure the two will like one another."

Alpine laughed and said, "I guess that is a part of Internet dating. Bonita, you are lovely and beautiful. I would like to get to know you, that is, if your feelings are mutual."

"The truth is I have never trusted Internet dating. I don't know how I let Jaza talk me into this. Let's see how tonight goes. After all, I am still alive."

"No, you didn't," Jaza said, holding both ears.

"I am still alive," Alpine repeated.

"She always said dating guys from the Internet could get you killed."

"You don't have a gun in your purse, do you?" Alpine asked, smiling at Bonita. "Different Bonita, so I don't have a phone number to trace. You might chop my head off."

The four of them laughed and talked for a while, then the couples began to chat separately. The evening was beautiful. Alpine said the end of the evening had come quickly and that he was excited about meeting her. He said that he could not wait for the next night so that they could have dinner. Bonita didn't respond. She found him quite charming, but was afraid of being so attracted to him.

∽

"Hello?"

"Good morning, Bonita. How are you?"

"I am fine. How are you this morning, Alpine?"

"After spending last evening with you, I'm doing wonderfully. I feel happy. What is your day looking like today?"

I am not spending everyday with the Internet man, Bonita thought. "I am preparing for church. After church, I'm going to prepare for the week. I have a new position at work and I have to strategize."

85

"I won't keep you from the Lord. He deserves your best. I hope that I will have the opportunity to spend more time with you. I did have an enchanting evening."

"It was a nice evening. Koffer and you did seem to be comfortable with one another. The evening was nice."

"Koffer and I are good friends. We have been friends for –"

"How did that happen?"

"The fact that we are friends?"

"Yeah."

"Koffer knew his lady was on the Internet trying to find a guy for her friend and that is how she met him."

"Ok."

"I was not sure about this Internet thing and I'm more surprised that I am attracted to you. I would like to get to know you. Will I see you again?"

"I am sure we will see one another again. Have you ever dated someone from the Internet?"

"Oh no. That Internet thing is not for me. I've told Koffer to stay away from ladies he's met on the Internet. Desperation, murder, you never know." Alpine was quiet for a moment and then, began laughing. His laughter was contagious and she joined in. After they both quieted, Bonita said, "Isn't this ironic? Neither of us are Internet daters, yet we are interested in one another."

"I'm glad to know that you are interested. But, to be truthful, I am looking for a lifetime mate," he said.

Lifetime mate, Bonita thought. *Didn't expect to hear that.*

"Bonita?"

"Yes, Alpine. I'm still here."

"I didn't scare you, did I?"

"I won't take to the aisle until I know more about you," she said.

"How about an early supper, so that we can get to know one another"

"Sure, but I have to go to church. I will call you when I get home."

"Ok, bye, my love. I will be waiting for your call."

Bonita looked into the phone incredulously, then put the phone to her face and said, "Goodbye Alpine."

◎

After church, Bonita was driving home, reviewing the Word that her pastor had preached. It was scary that it was almost the same sermon that Lloyd had spoken at the brunch two weeks ago about how the heart and mind are one and the same before God. *What shall I put in my mind Lord?* In the midst of her meditating, the phone rang.

"Hello?"

"Hi, Bonita. How are you?"

"Good morning, DJ Marl. What happened that I am on your mind this morning?"

"It is afternoon. I thought you would be out of church by now."

"I am. Time sure flies when you're having fun."

"Having fun?"

"Church was great today. I need to find my way back to the Lord's feet."

"Don't say that, I called to ask you out for breakfast. It is almost one, but I remember you like breakfast food."

"Ok, I'm impressed."

"Well, meet me at IHOP; it is right past the skillet."

"I was –"

"I'm pulling in now. I'll wait for you in the parking lot," he said before he disconnected the call. Bonita had just met Alpine, but she felt as though she was cheating.

DJ Marl and Bonita sat in IHOP for two hours. He shared his heart with her. After breakfast, she felt confused. She could hear Alpine saying, "I've been praying for a wife and I believe that she is you." She felt sad because she had made DJ Marl prove that he was not married or in a serious relationship. She had spent all of these years alone and now, she had to choose.

Before she made it home, the phone rang and it was Alpine.

"Hello, Bonita. I am calling so that we can put a time on dinner tonight."

"Ok, I am just leaving breakfast."

"Ok, what time is dinner? I want us to meet so that we can spend time getting to know one another."

That sounds familiar, she thought. "I am sure we both will work to make that happen. At this time, I have a new job and I will be spending time there. I am at the beginning of a building process. I hope that you can understand that."

"That's great; it gives us a reason to celebrate. Tonight, we will celebrate the occasion at Kris E's steakhouse."

"Sounds like the date is set. I don't want to be out too late. I have to rest up for the challenges ahead. Will 6 p.m. work for you?"

"Be there or be square."

They both laughed and hung up the phone.

∾

Bonita was there on time and Alpine was there one hour earlier than he reported.

"Hello Bonita, you look more beautiful than I remember," he said, as he kissed her hand.

Trying not to blush, she said, "Thank you, Alpine. Flattery will get you everywhere."

"I took the liberty of ordering champagne."

"This is quite a bottle! Thank you!"

"Here's the menu. I also ordered some hor d'oeuvres."

"You are so attentive and with the best. A girl can get used to this."

"That's what I 'm hoping for. So, how was your day? I thought about you at breakfast, lunch and siesta. I was trying to hurry the clock to get to touch your hand again." His strong eyes looked softly in hers as he gently held her hand. "I believe you are the woman that God has chosen for me. I can't close my eyes without thinking of you. I must be insane, more insane to say these things to you. Don't be afraid of this, Bonita. I know it will take you time to believe, but I will wait on you."

Bonita looked at him and sighed. *I can't believe my body is tingling in places that I do not wish to think about.* And, as he kissed her hand again with his tender, moist lips and gently batted his eyes, her nipples sprung at attention. Bonita sat speechless. He then began to feed her the hor d'oeuvres and held the glass to her mouth for her to drink. Dinner went wonderfully without Bonita saying much.

"When is the best time to call you?" he asked her.

"Whenever I am on your mind."

"Wow! Ok lady. I don't have that much time because you are always on my mind. I will try to refrain from calling that often. You are true to your name."

"Meaning?"

"You are beautiful. I will be calling. I believe you may be on my mind often. I have had such a wonderful evening."

"I have had a marvelous evening, as well. I will be waiting to hear from you."

∽

"Bonita, this is a four-way call." All three of her friends greeted her at once.

"You guys calling on Sunday? Have you been to church?"

"How was the date," Kate said, ignoring her. "Did you get some sex?"

"Kate, please! I don't know that guy. And if I did, you should never be easy with the guy you want."

"So, it is not just sex you want. You're looking for a relationship," Carmen responded.

"What are you talking about?"

"Sex is get a piece and go, Bonita. I can't say 'cum and go' 'cause that don't always happen, especially the first time," Carmen said. "And you're right," she said, addressing Kate.

"The two of them seemed pretty much into each other last night. I think we have something here, girls," Jaza said. "We may not be her only way out of the house soon."

Kate smacked her lips in the phone and said, "Get some soon. You are our supervisor now and you g'tting' off will be good for the atmosphere at work."

All of the girls laughed and Bonita said, "Speaking of the new job, I have to go now. I will see you guys tomorrow."

"Oh, heavens," Jaza said. "Wait, Bonita. What does new job and off the phone with us equate? Is it that you will not talk with us since you are our boss?"

"That statement does not include you girls at all. This job is bigger than you think. So much paperwork and more work to be done before the inspection."

"We will call you, Miss Important," Jaza said.

"Please don't act that way, Jaza. I can't do this alone. I need you girls to lead the staff in supporting me. That is the only way I can make it. I'm going to have a meeting with each of you so that we can set individual goals and make plans to grow a beautiful future for the patients and ourselves."

"Might be a little much for me," Jaza pouted.

"You sound like a commercial, but I'm behind you 100%," Carmen said.

Kate kicked in, "Me too, Bonita. I am with ya till the end."

Chapter 9

"*I* AM GLAD THAT YOU became the Director of Nurses here at the Wisdom Well Living Center because you understand my plight in this stinky place. I'm going to stay low-key until I get with this man and get out of Dodge," Jaza said.

Bonita's mind raced in frightened amazement. *Have mercy, Lord,* she thought. That statement made it difficult for her to discuss the guidelines for the job and expectations for change with Jaza. This girl had been her buddy in an intricate part in her quest for life, pushing her forward through the era of unknowing. Now that she was her supervisor, she wondered how she was going to stop the shopping and the two-hour lunches? Bonita took a deep breath, looked at Jaza and smiled. "Here is a cold soda. I knew you'd like it."

"You got me, girl. Hooking me up with my favorite drink. What's up?"

"Jaza, I would like you to know that I appreciate all that you have been in my life. I would not have made it this far on the job without your encouragement. Again, I thank you. This meeting is to explain the plan and create the map for us going forward at Wisdom

Well Nursing Home. In hopes that you understand now that I am the Director of Nursing, my role here and in our relationship here has changed. Our private lives, we are friends forever, I hope. But, the job is the job. As the supervisor, I must be true to the commitment of my job. Job and personal relationships are separate and the issues of each role have nothing to do with the other. When I speak to you as your supervisor, I do hope that you would respect me as such and work hard to meet our goals."

"What are you talking about? You already know that I am not going to get into all of that stuff. As long as no one is hurt –"

"Things have to change and I am depending on you to help me make things happen. You cannot walk off the unit or –"

"When did you read the book of right things to do on the job?"

"I have always followed the rules. I am building a better place for the residence here."

"You never stopped me from walking out before."

"I never participated in that, nor supported it. I was not your supervisor. Jaza, please don't make this difficult."

"If it was wrong, why didn't you report me? The knowing is just as bad."

"Whatever it was, I am not here to debate the past, but to build a future. We are here today to build a new and brighter future for the residence and ourselves."

Jaza's arms and head started moving as she spoke with a red face. "I'll be damned. You are not going to come in here pressuring us to be fools for this place like you are. I knew this fucking position would go to your head."

Bonita stepped back, realizing that Jaza was being loud enough for others to hear. Speaking quietly and firmly, she said, "Sit down and be quiet. I will not be able to spare your job here with this attitude. I did expect that you would be upset, but I did not expect this behavior from you. However, it will not be tolerated."

"You setting me up. You want to fire me. You want to put me in the place you left."

"No such thing! I want more for you. I want better for you. I want to help build your integrity so that you can have all that you want in life."

"My personal life has nothing to do with this remember."

"I am trying to bring you to understand self-growth. For the caliber of life you desire, you must develop integrity and ethics. I want you to be the best at what you do no matter your status in life."

"You are trying to be sure that I stay beneath you and not at your level. You're scared I would be better than you. You shouldn't burn your bridges because if Mrs. Wash has her way, you will be back on this side of the river."

Bonita's heart sunk, but she tried not to let it show. Discovering Mrs. Wash was Jean continued to be a struggle for her. Jaza needed to leave that one under the rock.

"Can we stay on the subject?"

"This is the subject. You know that I am here to pay my bills until someone else does."

"Look, if you are going to get where you want to go, you must go up a few levels. Your mentality has to change or a man with substance will not have you."

"Let me –"

"Be quiet and listen, I am not finished. On this job, you will clock in and out, you will not leave the premises for more than allotted time at lunch break and you will follow the job description and workflows. I will provide all that is needed for you to complete your job. My door is open for any of your needs on the job that will assist you in moving forward. Anything that needs to be said for our personal lives, we can discuss it outside."

Jaza stormed from the office, fuming and swearing. Bonita closed the door and leaned against it with her hands behind her back and tears in her eyes. She lowered her head down and prayed.

⟋⟍

Kate and Carmen met with their new Director of Nurses after lunch.

"Giving ya'll a great big hug. I am so glad you guys came in together. I need some support without stress." Both girls sat quiet, "You girls, ok?"

"Yes," they both said.

Bonita regrouped and went forward in a professional manner. "Hey guys, would you like a soda?

Both girls took one. Kate replied, "I just finished lunch, but I will take one anyway."

"We are starting up a program with major adjustments around here, but it is for the betterment of all of us. Are you girls in agreement?"

They both said yes.

"Great, let's get started. We are here to discuss changes and the new workflow that has been written by Mary Ann Hollinsworth and J. Stokes. To go along with the new workflow, that is if we have a consensus, we will need to update our job descriptions. That is where you ladies come in; I hope you are willing to help."

"Bonita, we are willing to do all that we can do to make you a success."

"Me too, Bonita," Carmen said. "I plan to be a true friend and work on this. I love you and want to show you that I am thankful."

"I knew you guys would make me happy. Okay, here's the plan."

The girls listened to the complete plan and added in their own positive input. Bonita couldn't help but feel pride in her friends.

"Bonita, can we talk a little bit about Jaza?" Carmen asked.

"Nothing negative towards her at all."

"Nothing against her," Carmen agreed.

"Ok, we can talk a little, but I am her supervisor and it would not be proper for me to hold conversations about other employees. If this will help us go forward and will stay in this room, go ahead, I'm listening."

"Bonita, Jaza's heart is broken. She said you did her like Mrs. Wash did you. Before you were on the new position for three weeks, you are trying to fire her. She said you pushed her," Kate said.

"Bonita, no one knows better than you and I how horrible it is for someone to come on the job and get an immediate dislike from the supervisor," Carmen said. "We are friends. We could have never believed you would do this to her. She needs this paycheck and you know that. I know she is flaky –"

"Ladies, I should not discuss another employee with you and after today, I never will."

"Bonita, I owe you my life. You can trust me," Kate said, with tears forming.

"Bonita, I promise, I am trying to help things along. I want this to be good for you," Carmen said.

"Kate, you don't owe me anything. Ladies, the position I have on this job has changed, my duties have changed and my responsibilities have changed. Most of all our working relationships have changed, as well. I called Jaza into the office as I did with you. Jaza didn't listen to anything I said. she was cursing loud enough for others to hear, standing up and wanting to fight and she is determined to continue along with the work ethics she has always performed. That can't work anymore. My boss is going to be watchful of how I handle her and all of you guys because I am your friend. Jaza has gone to Mrs. Stanzer to discuss me and to file a complaint against me and the changes I am presenting."

"I know she thinks that you told Mrs. Stanzer stuff about her," Carmen said. "She said that Mrs. Stanzer said if she was you, she would have fired her. She would not let Jaza explain why she thought that you were unfair. Mrs. Stanzer told her it is plain and simple, that you are now her superior and that you will give her instructions and make her daily assignments. She also told Jaza that if she doesn't think her friend can be her boss, then she would have to find another job because you were not going anywhere."

"That sounds very harsh, but what she didn't tell you is that that was her second trip to Mrs. Stanzer. I never went once. But, for Jaza and you guys, I am a different kind of supervisor and we will take care of the patients."

"Bonita, I am sorry if she disrespected you," Kate said.

"I am going to work hard," Carmen said. "You will be proud of me; I want you to look good."

"We will work harder together to make this a better place for the residents to live and for us to work. I will make sure that the Wisdom Well shows us that they do appreciate us. Call me. Maybe we can go to H and R Cafeteria for supper tonight," Bonita said.

"Can Jaza come?" Kate asked.

"I do not want to be without her," Bonita said.

∽

When the day was over, Bonita left the building and headed to her car. Before she could open the door, Jaza walked up.

"We are outside, friends now right?" Jaza asked.

"Right, Jaza. Are you ok?"

"I guess you feel like 'Ms. I Got It All'. Is this what you wanted an RN Position for?"

"I am sorry that you don't understand. We are in a new —"

"Bonita, I feel like you betrayed me."

"Jaza, you have misunderstood the entire situation. I just cannot allow you to go on doing the wrong thing."

96

"The wrong thing. You would not know anything of what I do if you didn't pretend to be my friend."

"I am your friend, but my role at work has changed in your life."

"Role my ass. You just want brownie points with Mrs. Stanzer."

"I have made my brownie points. That is why I have the position I have."

"Ass-kisser. Brown-noser."

"Call it what you may, but I won't stoop to that level with you."

"Stoop to where I am? You were the one with no phone, living in a shelter."

"What does that have to do with this situation?"

"This is what it has to do with it. I should have left your hungry, broke ass just like that. This would not be my problem now if I had."

"Your problem is with you, honey. If I had died of starvation, you would still be the irresponsible person you are today."

"Irresponsible?"

"Yes, irresponsible and your poor work ethics."

"How dare you!"

"Dare and swear if you want. You did not know me or anything about me when we met and you proudly stated how you neglect the patients and steal from the job."

"So, you want to fight. Steal from the job? I never stole from the job."

"Walking off the job for hours on the clock is stealing. The next time I see you do that, I will punch your card for you."

"Punch my card and I will call EEOC."

"I will do better than punch your card. I will cover your post and fire you for stealing."

"I believe you, the bitch that you are."

"I will be a lot of things, but I will not be one of those."

"Whatcha gonna do?"

"I see where this is going. I will end this conversation with you, Jaza. Have a good day."

"Drive across the light and die, Bonita!" Jaza screamed out. Bonita's heart sunk.

Can't believe she'd say that, she thought. She drove off and it felt like the longest drive home she had ever had. Alpine had been a blessing. She had only known him for five days and she didn't know how she would make it a day without him. *He will be my peace at this moment. Lord, thank You for Alpine.*

When she got home, she lay down heavily on her couch and called Alpine.

"Hello, how are you today, my Internet man, Alpine?"

"I am doing so wonderful now that I have heard your voice."

"You are growing on me, too. I think you have me hooked."

"I hope in the best kind of way. If you look at the details of how we met, we technically did not meet on the Internet. First, I should ask you how your day was."

"I have known you for a short time, but you make me smile, so the only part of my day that counts is you. So, I am having the best day at this moment. How about that?"

"That is the answer to my dream, beautiful. I have been thinking all day about making you a permanent part of my life."

"Oh, permanent?"

"Don't be afraid. My parents met and were married three weeks later. I am going home in four months for their fifty-year anniversary."

"Maybe I will go with you. I want to know more about you before we schedule the important life-long covenant of marriage."

"I know enough about you."

"What is your favorite color? How do you respond to anger?" Bonita asked.

"Good questions. My favorite color is gold. I like its brilliance. And I try not to get angry."

"But what happens if you do become angry? Have you ever hit a female or called her a bad name?"

"This is the first time I've been asked these questions. I like that. The thought of being married doesn't excite you? You're looking to share life. I am loving you more and more. To answer your questions, I have never called anyone out of their name. I do have self-control. If I'm in business and I am angry, I call for a recess because time away from a sticky matter gives one a chance to rethink and regroup. At home, I would ask to move the discussion to a later time for the same reason. I would try to move on to a more pleasant subject because I think if we were to walk away angry, ugly feelings would settle in our hearts and mind. How would you deal with that?"

"I would like it. I don't like a domineering man, but I like a man that leads and is strong. I would want to trust his judgment and feel safe and cared for all at the same time. By the way, my favorite color is purple."

They continued their conversation until 12:30 in the morning, discussing their lives, likes and dislikes. Bonita thought that she could actually feel herself falling in love.

Wow, I have a serious dilemma, am I married. How can I get rid of that curse of a situation and move on? I have a new life, my own real life for the first time in thirty-three years. Maybe I will have to go back to settle it all. I will get Mom to go with me. She hates those people and would do anything to free me from them.

Chapter 10

*B*Y LUNCH TIME ON Wednesday, Bonita was worn out. The residents were excited like it was Christmas. Though the employees complained with raging attitudes, she felt a sense of self-satisfaction from them over the residents' joy. The next day was Thursday but Bonita decided that today would be her Friday. *Like hell if I come to this place another day without detoxifying my mind.*

Bonita felt stressed and stretched thinking to herself, *Man, this place in life is the new definition of insanity. Nothing no one has ever said to me could have prepared me for this experience. This is like doing flips in space with no place to land my cartwheels, or like a ballerina in orbit pushing, but never getting her pirouette around. Can my rocket ship land on earth again? Amazed is not a word to use while thinking of this week. I never dreamed life could feel like this. I don't know what to think about my not knowing what to feel. It is good and bad, I suppose. Just so much paperwork and fighting through others' emotions. I won't call Alpine today, we talked until after midnight last night. I just want to get drunk and pass out.*

After work, on the way home, Bonita stopped off at the package store to buy a bottle of Rose Courvoisier and she pulled in a nearby Burger King parking lot to drink it, trying to stop her mind from thinking and her heart from hurting. She didn't know how to describe to herself what her heart was going through at this time. She prayed all the way home, begging the Lord not to let her get a DUI.

She luckily managed to get home without a ticket and she sat in the car, gathering my senses and stabilizing herself. Distracted, Bonita walked through the parking lot and up to the door of her apartment, thinking in the back of her mind, *Lord, don't let me fall.* As she dug in her purse for the keys, she thanked the Lord for not letting her fall or allowing anyone to see her this drunk. She laughed at herself because she had never drank this much alcohol in such a short time. Her head was spinning in a funny way. Once the door was open, she threw everything in and thought to myself, *I'll make a run to my bed. I just want to lie in my heaven tonight. I'll wake up tomorrow and try to sort this out.* She took a running start through the door and slammed it behind, but a hand slammed against the door and she heard a voice say, "Bonita."

She turned and her heart hit the floor before her knees did. That moment seemed like a lifetime to her. The last person she expected to see – Bruce, her estranged husband – was standing in front of her in her living room.

"Bonita, I've missed you, Bonita!"

Bonita began to tremble in fear, tears rolled from her face and terror rolled down her heart. She shrieked, "Am I going to die?"

"Baby, no! I came to say I'm sorry. Sorry for ever hurting you."

"Ever," she squealed.

"Every time. Look, I've changed. I'm not going to ever hurt you again. I know I can't simply walk into your life and be your husb –"

"Are we divorced?"

"Are we divorced? Love of my life, I would never divorce you."

Bonita began to cry, saying, "Lord Jesus, help me. I want him and everything about him to go away."

Bruce began to cry. He held his heart and his right hand out to her. "Baby, what do you mean? I don't want to go away. I love you. I promise, I won't hurt you. I will never hurt you again. Please, can I help you?"

She sat on her knees, lifeless and drained. She had no power to fight for her life. *Alpine, what will I tell Alpine?* Her husband reached down and picked her up from the floor.

"Baby, I miss your soft touch, your sweet smell. I miss you."

Afraid to speak, she laid staring into the space of her small apartment as he pulled her clothing from her body, waist down. She did not dare say anything because he had always felt entitled to rape her anytime he wanted to because she was his wife. Grime and shame is what she felt as he gyrated on top of her. She thanked God that he didn't go to her bed. He took her in his arms and fell asleep with her in his arms on the sofa.

The morning sun beamed down into Bonita's eyes, causing pain and blurred vision. Fear gripped her very being. There was only one way out of the apartment and that was past him through the front door.

"You're up, Bonita. I am preparing breakfast for us."

Why did I call off before my alcohol binge? I should have thought that out longer, she thought, as she looked in the mirror. She stared into her own soul and she looked hard for an answer or understanding to the catastrophe that she was facing this morning. *Where did he come from and how did he find me? Is this real? She felt so numb.*

"What are you doing in my kitchen?!" she suddenly screamed out.

"Preparing breakfast and I am done. Breakfast is served, come eat."

"When did you start cooking?"

"Sister Garden taught me. I wanted to learn something that would convince you that I had changed if I would see you again. She is leading the women ministry since you left us. She has them living holy."

"Are you saying that I was not effective in leading the women in the congregation to holiness?" Even in her anger, Bonita understood that she needed to be very careful not to provoke the violent man who lived inside of Bruce.

Very carefully, Bruce swallowed and answered, "Baby, no, that is not at all what I meant. You hurt me when you left, but your leaving devastated a lot of the women. "

"Do you blame me for leaving?"

"Bonita I am trying to say that your leaving was difficult for the church. You are quite a powerful influence in our lives and your leaving created a great void. You have such an influence over me. It is overpowering and controlling. I couldn't handle the way everyone loved you. The men would often say to me, 'I wish my wife was like yours.'"

"Do you blame me for leaving?"

"I do wish you had handled things differently. Sometimes, I was so intimidated by your love for the people and I didn't have that —"

"Why did you abuse me so? You beat me, choked me and locked me in the closet. Was I supposed to live with that?"

"Bonita," Bruce said, beginning to cry. "I am haunted by the memories of you crawling around the floor because of me. I am tormented by the day that you backed away from me like a hurt, beaten pup." He fell to the floor, holding her knees. "Baby, please, please forgive me. Bonita, I am sorry. I am so sorry. Please forgive me. I know that I could never erase the past. I was an animal, Please forgive me."

Bonita stood with her arms folded and said, "Did Sister Garden tell you to say those things? Bruce, I forgave you when I walked out of the door. I knew for me to go forward, I had to leave the death of unforgiveness behind me. Is that what this is all about?"

"What, Bonita? What do you mean?"

"This. Is it all about you being able to leave with you –"

"No, baby. I know there is nothing I can say or do that will make you fathom the love that I have for you and the pain that I feel inside."

"Right."

"Baby, I'm sorry."

"For reasons unknown to me, I believe a part of some of that somewhere."

"I could not live with what I have done to you. I have been hospitalized and had counseling."

"What was the doctor's advice to you?"

"Advice about?"

"Advice about me, Bruce."

"I think you are asking about a diagnostic conclusion that was given for me."

"You did go to psychiatrist, if you can say that, Bruce. Call it what you want, But no, I 'm not asking about you. It's not all about you."

"Why are you being so hard to me?"

"Dude, you beat the hell out of me for every meal of the day. What do you want from me?"

"I thought you forgave me?"

"I have, but I'm not a fool. You still haven't lost it. I'm not afraid to die. It was my mistake to think that I had escaped the death of your hand."

With his face in his hands, Bruce dropped his head in shame. "I can't undo it love. Baby, I am sorry I –"

"The doctor's prognosis must have been deep."

"I was diagnosed with some personality disorder. The doctor did say it would take much discipline, but without discipline, I would always be prone to the extreme."

"So, that means at any minute, you can get up from there, beat my ass and tie me up, huh?"

"Bonita, this has not been easy for me. I had a nervous breakdown being without you."

The sides of Bonita's mouth went up and she laughed, "Yeah, sure, that's all."

"I love you. When I went to the hospital, I gave up the office of Pastor."

"You mean to tell me you made that decision on your own?"

"Word was out in the church the true reason you left. The women in the congregation did not feel comfortable without you there to discuss our personal lives. I don't know who put our personal business out. The board made a written request and I signed the agreement, then signed myself into treatment."

"And I am supposed to feel what?"

Silence filled the room for a long moment.

"Baby, I was sick and I think we could have handled the situation in a different way. I needed your help."

"And from what you are saying and not saying, your ass is still sick and I am no safer now than I was then."

"Please believe me. Mental illness is as real as the asthma your daddy suffered from. I'm being treated."

"Convince me by taking responsibility for your actions and stop using 'I'm sick' as an excuse to destroy my life. And stop trying to say things that you think will hurt me because I am immune now. There are consequences for grown people's actions."

"Bonita, I take medicine now."

"What medicine let me see the medicine?"

"I didn't bring it with me. I won't stay here long."

"Leave while I am still alive. I am not afraid to die, but it is just as I said I always knew I would die at your hand. If you don't mean me any harm, leave," Bonita said.

"I don't want to leave on negative terms. Can we watch a movie?"

He doesn't have his medicine; this dude has got to be crazy, she thought.

"Let's watch Forrest Gump," he said. "My opinion is that it is funny and calm. Jenny had a baby for Forrest and she stayed with him until she died."

"We have watched three movies and I am sleepy. Tonight I am going to sleep in my bed"

"Am I invited to your bed for the night?"

"I would prefer not." *Lord, my only save place in the world is my bed.*

"OK, all I want is for you to love me like I love you."

Bonita went to her room and laid in bed, thinking, *you would be dead if I loved you the way you love me.* The suave, charming guy in the living room, she knew him. That's the guy she met. She knew that he would charm her until he could get close enough to cut her neck off. The 'I'm sorry' begging guy, she didn't know him. He was new to her. She tapped the wall, whispering 'help' throughout the night, hoping her neighbors would be home to hear.

The next morning after breakfast, the phone rang. *Carmen or Kate to my rescue.* Bruce jumped over me to get the phone and he turned it off. *Welcome back, real Bruce.*

"Bonita, we need this time together."

"For what reason?"

"That we may become friends again."

"Ok, Bruce. Please don't get rough. That frightens me."

"I won't," he said, as he kissed his cheek.

During the day, she tried to interest him in many sightseeing tours and restaurants to visit, but Bruce had an excuse each time to stay in and not leave the apartment. She stayed low-key and turned in early because she had seen the old Bruce peep out a few times during the day on Saturday. But, she knew that once they left the apartment for church on Sunday, she would be home free. She tapped the wall again during the night, but again, got no response.

After breakfast Sunday morning, she picked up the dishes and said, "Let's get ready for church."

Bruce was indignant. "We are not going to church today."

"What?" she asked, gently, aware of his rising anger. "I can't believe you don't want to go to church."

"From the day I married you, you have wanted to leave me. I was never good enough for you. You're still mad because I am not your dad."

"What does that have to do with us going to church?"

"You don't care about going to church; you are trying to get away from me." Bruce suddenly slapped Bonita to the floor and began crying. "See! You see what you made me do?!"

"Bruce, you have not taken your medicine, you don't have –"

"That's why I never liked sharing my secrets with you!"

Bonita saw that Bruce was quickly losing control and she tried to think fast. "Bruce, you are going to hurt me. Be disciplined, Bruce."

She didn't know if she should fight for her life or give up and allow him to kill her. The two sat in the living room for hours. Bonita was too afraid to move and she didn't know what was going on his mind. Periodically, he would start to cry and sometimes, he would look at her to say, "I am so sorry, I love you. Please forgive me. Other times, he'd look at her with venom in her eyes and sneer, "You are selfish. You never took the time out to try to learn how to treat me." But each time the phone rang, he'd become enflamed with anger. Bonita continued to hum hymns and spiritual songs.

"Stop it. Stop humming and singing."

She fell asleep off and on throughout the day and when she suddenly heard a knock at the door, she didn't know what time it was. She heard Kate scream out, "Bonita, are you in there? Are you ok?"

Bonita screamed back, "Go get help Kate! I need help!"

Bruce immediately flew into a rage and started yelling. He jumped up up and started slapping and punching Bonita around the room. The more Kate screamed for Bonita, the harder Bruce punched her. The fear in Kate's voice gave Bonita the strength to fight back.

"Do you think I am afraid of your little friends," Bruce hissed through his clenched teeth.

"Do you think I am afraid of you killing me? I left you because I couldn't take any more of this. I knew the real you was still there inside, Bruce," Bonita hissed back.

"It has to be you. I have not done anything like this since you left."

"I will not take the responsibility of you acting up and trying to blame it on me. It is a damn shame that you don't take responsibility for your silly ass actions. Get a hold of yourself."

Bruce threw a lamp and shouted, "Where does all of the cursing come from? The church should hear you now. You don't sound like that sweet Bonita everyone wanted to arrest me over."

Bruce became visibly angrier the more he yelled. He began to throw objects at her. The two had been fighting for approximately thirty minutes when Bonita finally picked up a crystal picture and smashed it across his head, cutting his chest. At that point, the fighting became fiercer and the two knocked over furniture. Bruce suddenly yanked off his belt and began strangling her with it. Bonita saw fury in Bruce's eyes and she felt in her heart that this was the moment her husband was going to kill her and she quickly seized control of the war.

She then heard a loud knocking at the door, followed by a series of shrill screams. She knew it was Kate and she didn't want her to come in and find her dead body. Her heart began pounding rapidly and she somehow managed to throw Bruce off and free her body. Bruce bellowed and he looked like a monster from a horror movie.

"Look what you've done! You cut me, you bitch! I'm bleeding! You finally got your wish to make the world think I'm the bad guy. This is what I hate about you!" Bruce screamed and bounded like a gorilla toward his wife. Bonita ran toward the recliner, when she pushed it into Bruce's path, she saw the mini ax she had forgotten she'd placed there for protection and threw it at him. The ax whizzed right into his skull and he fell to the floor. He immediately screamed and fell to his knees.

"Don't pull it out! Oh my God, oh my God. Don't touch it, Bruce!"

Lloyd kicked in the door just in time to see the chair fall over and Bruce falling to his knees. He ran into the bloody scene with Kate and the police. Bonita fell to her knees, as well, pointing and trying to speak, but she became overwhelmed and she passed out.

Chapter 11

SHE LAY LISTENING INQUISITIVELY to the sounds and voices in the environment trying to decipher my location. She prayed in her head, *Lord, please let me lie here and if I have to wake up, don't let it be now.* She felt like she had a taste of heaven, then had immediately been thrust into the fires of hell. If there is any such thing, it was as if her emotions were having strokes and seizures at that moment. Her face hurt badly and my head felt swollen. My body was numb and felt like she had been beaten by Muhammad Ali. She honestly never thought that she would have to live through that kind of experience again and to think, a few minutes more and she would have been dead.

Lord, I want my wonderful world with Alpine. That's all I want. Oh God, where is Bruce and is he ok?

Bonita stopped thinking so that she would hear the voices of people she knew and what they were saying. She heard Sigrid's voice saying, "Arrest her? What do you mean?"

A strange male voice answered, "She may be arrested."

Kate and Sigrid sobbed in the background and she heard, "She can't go to jail!"

"Arrested? Arrested for what, may I ask, Officer?" The person asking this sounded like Lloyd.

"What is your relationship to the suspect, sir?"

Sigrid and Kate continued to cry. Lloyd nervously said, "Suspect? She is the victim, for sure. This man beat her repeatedly."

Suspect, what hell what is going on? God, I can't wake up. They will take me to jail.

"I was the officer who arrived at the apartment. This man kicked the door in."

The first unknown male voice said, "I am the officer who rode with Mr. Bruce Advent to the hospital. He told us that Mrs. Advent cut him with glass and attempted to cut his head off with an ax. He has lacerations across his left upper arm and his torso and the ax had been lodged in his head. He attempted to escape when the door was kicked in."

"Officer, he told you that with an ax in his head," Lloyd said.

"Sir, he was coherent when he went into surgery. The doctor came back to report his death to us five minutes ago. There is a detective assigned to this case. He will officially questions and arrest Mrs. Advent. She, nor either of you, are required to answer questions without a lawyer present,"

"Sir, I was the one who kicked in the door. She did not look aggressive to me at that time"

Sigrid and Kate continued to cry loudly and Lloyd said, "Sir she is not conscious. She passed out at the house and has not been conscious since. She has been beaten beyond recognition. I assure you that there is more to this case than his side of the story. Shouldn't all of the evidence pertaining to the case be collected before she is labeled the suspect and arrested?"

The room sounded silent for a moment before Lloyd spoke again. "Yes, it may be that she had been beat with objects for a while. I was told that she has not seen this man you are calling her husband for years."

Sigrid's said, "She was here in this town running from him. He was an abusive husband and she feared for her life. Somehow, he found her."

"The officer said I will need you guys to speak to the detective when..."

Bonita had heard enough. She turned everything in the outside world off and began to pray again.

Lord, go to jail. I can't go to jail. How did this happen? I won't survive in jail. Lord, I thought I was doing everything you wanted. It was Sister Garden's idea for me to be a nurse. The motive was for me to get away, but I have been the best nurse to your people that I knew how. How could you let this happen to me, Jesus? Show yourself strong and deliver me one more, please.

Bonita stopped praying to listen to the voices in the room.

"I am Detective David Madison of the homicide division. I am looking for Bonita Advent."

"Bonita," Lloyd said, "is room 512, but she cannot speak; she is unconscious."

"She is not guilty of anything, Officer. She has been beaten to the point that she does not even look like herself," Sigrid said, sternly.

Bonita could hear the group enter the room.

"Mrs. Advent," he said, touching her softly. She didn't respond to his voice or touch.

"I will need to question anyone that was at the scene."

"I was the person that kicked in the door, Lloyd said. "I saw Mr. Advent fall to the floor with the ax in his head. Bonita was across the room and I went over to pick her from the floor and she passed out."

"Will she have to wear shackles?" Sigrid asked in a shaky voice.

"I have seen his kind before. If she retains a lawyer, it could be very easy to prove her case. That is, if all that you are saying is true."

"Is she a suspect? Will she have to wear shackles?" Sigrid's voice squealed again.

"Ma'am, at this time, there have been formal charges levied against Mrs. Advent."

"What does that mean?" Sigrid cried.

The conversation continued for a while longer and she heard the room clearing out. She peeked through her closed eyes and saw that only Sigrid remained. She sat at the edge of the bed, with her head down and she appeared to be deep in prayer.

Bonita softly whispered, "I'm scared, Sigrid."

Sigrid jumped and screamed.

"Shhh!! Don't tell anyone I'm awake. I'm not trying to go to jail yet."

The nurse suddenly walked in and asked, "Is everything ok? What can I help you with?"

Bonita lay quiet and still, as if she was in a coma.

"It all becomes overwhelming at times, I will be ok," Sigrid said to the nurse.

"This must be hard on you, seeing your daughter like this."

"I am not her mom."

"Oh, we thought you were her next of kin. She cannot communicate and we need someone to legally manage her care. Do you know her mom or next of kin? We will need to have that information ready."

"I do not have that information with me, but I can have it ready at the desk tonight."

"We would appreciate that. Call me if you need anything."

Bonita waited until the nurse was completely out of the room before she whispered again.

"Sigrid, I am afraid. I don't want to go to jail. I can't, I won't make it."

"Bonita, do you have a lawyer? You do have a bail and we are trying to get money together. Do you have any"

"I have some. How much is the bail?"

"You have been charged with manslaughter and domestic violence and the bail is $25,000."

"How much have you collected?"

"I have about $9, 000 between myself, Lloyd, Mrs. Stanzer, Kate, Carmen and the owner of Wisdom Well. We did not discuss this matter with anyone else in the building."

"All of those people know... Oh God, I never want to go back to that place again. You will have to go to my home to get my checkbook. I have $15, 000 to my name. I can't write or sign a check since I'm in a coma. Can you guys come up with the other $1000?"

"Bonita, we will because if you don't, the police will come to shackle you and have guards here around the clock."

"This is my mom's phone number for the nurse. But, call her first to tell her only an outline of what has happened. She will die when this is all over."

"When are you going to talk to everyone else? I will be careful what I say around comatose people. You never know what they hear."

"Mrs. Jackson taught me about catatonia, as well, and the Lord has given me the strength to maintain it."

"I am going to give this phone number a call at the nurse's station."

෴

Sigrid came in the next morning at 8:30 a.m. "I went down to pay your bail this morning. Now, we need money for a good lawyer."

This was Sigrid's first evening and night away. Bonita was relieved, but she didn't feel like talking this morning. She didn't respond and Sigrid sat there, praying. Bonita awakened to a strong negative presence at the bedside and she called out, "Who's there?"

"I came to see if you were dead or alive."

"Jean," Bonita whispered and she opened her eyes, trying to hide her tremendous fear. "Are you going to kill me since I am not dead?"

"And rot in the place that been cut out for you to rot in, I don't think so. My soul would have been happy if you were dead, but watching you being killed softly will give me ecstasy."

"What good would me being dead do for your soul?"

"Because I would finally come out on top."

"Who told you I was here?"

"The newspaper said you killed your husband and that you can get up to life in person." Jean laughed heartily. "Daddy should be here to see his golden child go to jail for murder."

"I thank God for Daddy's love. You've been the richest all of our lives, but envy and jealousy kept you from reaping your benefits, Jean."

"What benefits?"

"You're beautiful and intelligent. You grew up with your life as your own. You are a nurse because that is what you wanted to do. I became a nurse to free me from my marital prison. You have a husband that loves you and children. You have it all, Jean. Be grateful and live your life."

"I will after I see you suffer."

"I had a picture perfect life through your eyes, right? The grass is not always greener on the other side, Jean and harboring grudges rots your soul."

"Your grass was green enough to attract my dad away from me and to draw attention to yourself from every place I have seen you."

"Let me tell you, sister, what you truly saw. You had your life to live. Our dad and my mom chose everything for me until Daddy died. I had no choice in my matters. When my marriage was over, I did not go to the security of home where everything was waiting for me because I wanted to do my life. I knew I would be at rock bottom because that was the only place I could have a life of my own. Don't spend all of your life trying to make mine miserable. Because the truth is you are miserable and making yourself more miserable every minute you focus on me. You will not be going to my funeral any time soon. I won't go to jail, Jean. Jesus is my source."

Sigrid walked into the room and asked, "What's going on?"

"I was coming to pay my respects," Jean said, and she walked out without turning around to look back or say goodbye.

"Respects? What was that about Bonita?"

"She came hoping I was dead, Sigrid."

"What?"

Bonita shook her head and moved on. "My concern right now is that I don't go to jail. I am afraid and I need to sleep. I'm scared." Tears began to fall down her face.

Sigrid wiped her eyes and said a prayer. She then got up and went into the bathroom. Bonita heard her say, "Hello, my name is Sigrid. I am a very close friend of Bonita's" before Sigrid closed the door. After about 10 minutes, she came out and sat on the bed next to her.

Sigrid returned to sit by the bed, "Bonita, that was your mom. I told her everything that has happened."

"Was she upset?"

"I don't know what you heard, but yes, she was as upset as any mother would be. She wants to come. She is handling it. I told her that we have the money to post bail and that Mrs. Stanzer found a great attorney."

"She did?!"

"Yeah, don't get too excited, though. We're going to need $15,000 to retain him. But, I think your mom is going help us with the money."

Bonita sighed. "Well, I am just relieved that my mommy will be here. She will make everything better. Sigrid, please make sure the attorney is good. I don't want to go to jail."

Chapter 12

"GOD IS SO GOOD to me."

Bonita breathed a long sigh and settled into the car. "What a great mode of transportation, 1965 Mustang. To tell you the truth, this is how you caught Mr. Emmanuel."

"Stop it, Bonita," Sigrid laughed. "Actually, he knew it was a lifetime desire of mine and he brought it home one day five years ago just because."

"That's love, isn't it? He must have inherited it because this had to cost a pretty penny."

"Emmanuel came fixed financially and because of that, I 'm ok now myself. I have a nice inheritance for my children and grandchildren."

"Oh, don't tell Jaza that. The thought of marrying wealthy and having to have a job would kill that girl at a ripe young age." They both laughed harder.

"Speaking of Jaza, I hope you are up for company."

"Company? Like who? Where is my mom?"

"Your mom is at your apartment, preparing your favorite foods. We have the apartment fixed up nice and a few of your close friends are coming for dinner."

"Close friends? Who, Kate and Carmen? And don't leave out Lloyd and his wife."

"Jaza asked if she can come and bring a dish."

"Is she coming to see that I am still alive, too?"

"Too? What are you talking about?"

"My sister came to the hospital to see if I was still alive and if she would get the finally victory over me. Don't mention that to my mom, please."

"Too much new information, Bonita. What sister?"

"I discovered that my wicked witch of the east is Mrs. Wash herself. Do you remember the day in the hospital when you walked in and she walked out saying, 'I came to pay my respects'?"

"Goddamn, I'm about to faint. How in God's earth can that be?"

"We did not like each other from a very young age and we did all we could to destroy one another every time the opportunity arose. I didn't have to do anything much to break her eggs because I owned the golden goose."

"I am afraid to ask for an explanation. How did you guys get to be sisters? How could you not have recognized one another?"

"She recognized me immediately. I was her lifetime terror. Our father was married to her mother, who was his mistress and he deserted them once my mom became pregnant with me. I was his dream child and they were his nightmare family. I did not know who Jean was until she came in for the kill in the middle of hallway B and, as it had always been, I had the power of the sting that would knock life from her. How could any of this be rectified?"

Sigrid remained silent, frozen in shock.

"Enough of that," Bonita said, dismissing it all. "I want to thank you guys from the bottom of my heart for all that you've done for me.

It was gracious of my mom to pay and the apartment management to allow you all to move me into a new apartment."

"It is on the other side of the complex, so you don't have to go home the old way or think of any of it again. We didn't bring the living room furniture. We brought new furniture for the living room."

"Where did you get money for that?"

"Bonita, I have not been back to work since the night this all happened. I have been taking care of you only. Emmanuel knew how important you are to me and he was happy that I had someone to take care of. When I mentioned the idea of getting new furniture and a new apartment, we went out, brought it and had it delivered. I am sure you will love it. Your mom said she would have done it. Emmanuel thanked her for sharing you."

Bonita was teary-eyed. "I thank God for His favor. Thank you for loving me. It is good to be home. I am so glad that Mom handled this all in love. She is the best."

Bonita walked into the apartment and there was the furniture she did previously tell Sigrid she was saving for. "This is so beautiful. Thank you! Thank you, Mom!"

"I have the bed turned down. I'm sure you can't wait to lie in your bed."

"I want to look in the mirror through my eyes to see the brand new me."

"Are you ok, Bonita?" Sigrid asked.

With a serious expression, she answered, "This is the best time of my life."

"About everything. I want to know if your heart is ok about everything."

"If you guys are thinking about the Bruce situation, I am ok. I hope this doesn't sound cold, but it was either him or me. If it had not been now, it would have been later. I am sure my dad had no idea he was marrying me off to a bonafide crazy man."

"I assure you he had not an idea of Bruce's nature, nor Mrs. Garden," her mom said. "It was best to happen after he died. They dared not try any of that while he was living."

"It is amazing that a person could hide serious mental illness without the world knowing."

"The world doesn't know, but the person knows and they try to hide it. His mom got it before he married me," Bonita said.

"Got what? What do you mean?"

"He could not have beaten his mom the way he beat you," her mom said. "Wait. Do you want to talk about this? It is a little deeper than I thought. I am sorry, I don't want to upset you. How did your dad not know? What did he do to my child?"

"It's ok; I need to talk about it, but don't be angry with Dad, Mom. He had no idea of the dysfunction."

"Have you forgiven Bruce?"

"I think I have. He used his mental situation as a crutch to abuse women."

"Why would his mom allow him to marry you knowing he was beating her?"

"Pride and to cover family sin, I suppose. Their family is the church family of the town."

"Bonita, he didn't show any signs of mental illness while you were dating?"

"Huh," Bonita smiled. "My marriage to Bruce was arranged between my Dad and his best friend, Mrs. Garden, Bruce's mother. He did not show any signs of abuse toward me until after my dad was dead in his grave. This is why I believe he knew he had a problem, but was in control of it. His was crazy, not stupid."

"I'll agree with that," her Mom said. "His mom called while I was in the hospital to apologize for everything."

"Did she take responsibility for everything her son had done?"

"No, she took responsibility for what she had done. She did introduce my dad to my mom. She knew her son was abusive, but could not expose him without exposing and destroying her family. She cooperated with the investigators on my case, thank God! You would not guess what now."

"Oh God, there's more?" Sigrid grabbed her head.

"The pastor of the family church now is Bruce, Jr. – a son he fathered when he was thirteen that I had not met, nor knew existed. One thing I have to say on Mrs. Garden's behalf is that she orchestrated the church deal to pay my tuition for nursing school. I didn't have a desire to be a nurse, but she said that would be my only way out."

"That entire family is crazy." Bonita's mother said as she warmed the food and set the table. "I am sorry this nightmare happened to you. Why didn't you call me Bonita?"

"I could have called at any time to end the madness. I didn't because life itself had her stressed out and the stress of my pain may have taken you under. Most of all, I handled it myself. For the first time in my life, I am doing my own life. I have taken leadership and ownership of my destiny. In that sense, it was worth the beatings."

"Nothing is worth a man beating my child. We'll talk about that another time."

"I don't know what I am feeling at this time. I guess only you could understand that," Sigrid said.

"Bonita, I will be leaving first thing in the morning, but I will return before your court appearance."

"Ok, mom, I am sure you have a reason to leave and I am looking forward to you coming back. I thank God you guys are my parents."

"Why that now?"

"It is nothing like having a dad who takes care of me including after he is gone and a mom who is at my side whenever I call. Your food is good, Mom. What's for dinner tomorrow?"

"I made a roast and baked sweet potatoes. The meal is pot luck. Everyone is bringing the dish you like them to prepare. The idea was Jaza's, believe it or not. She instructed everyone to make extra, so that we will be able to leave you a few meals and you won't have to cook for a while," Sigrid exclaimed.

"Come, come. We have to get you beautiful for your big day tomorrow."

୬୭

Lloyd and his wife were the first guess to arrive after, of course, Sigrid and Mr. Emmanuel, who had come over from church. She was surrounded by her friends and she felt the most refreshed than she been in more than a month. They played Monopoly, Scramble, Scattergories and Dominos. They ate until they were falling over. The barbeque red fish and the crawfish that Monica made was the best. Bonita didn't have to do anything. The dishes were washed and put away and the apartment was clean. Everyone left but Jaza and Bonita didn't know what to say.

"Bonita I put this gathering together as a token of my appreciation. And I stayed back to say I am sorry."

"Pick your head up. You have nothing to be ashamed of. If you are doing this because of what happen –"

"No, not at all. It was Koffer who opened my eyes."

"Koffer? What did he do?"

"He really likes you, Bonita. He asked me where you were and I said in the hospital. He wanted to go see you and I said no. He found the newspaper article about the incident and read it. I told him that wasn't you because didn't know that last name. And I knew you weren't married."

"You could have said my new position was taking all my time."

"Let me apologize."

"I am sorry, go ahead."

"When I had someone else as the maid of honor in my wedding, he would take no more evasive answers. You were right to care enough about me to assist in building my character. Koffer told me he was willing to send me to school, but not before I complete the school of life."

"School of life? What does that mean?"

"He says that my job had taken care of me for three years and it was as if I was stealing the money and my welfare was on the back of the institution."

"He said that to you, Jaza?"

"Yes, he did. My feelings were so hurt. Lots of what he said was as if you were standing right there. I have to stay on the job until I love it. But, he is going to give me the wedding I want."

"Let's talk about the fun –"

"You didn't say if you would be my maid of honor."

"Of course! I would be honored! Have you planned all of the festivities?"

"I have a meeting with you guys next week."

"Which day next week? I have to go to court on Wednesday and this is a very stressful time for me. After next Wednesday, I'm going to be ok, my lawyer promised. Can it be Thursday or Friday, preferably Saturday or Sunday evening. My mom will be gone. Oh, and Carmen and Kate in the wedding?"

"They offered to wear the colors to serve as ushers the day of the wedding."

"What are the colors?"

"Tangerine, chocolate, a little cream and a trim of gold."

"Ok, nice."

"You must see the colors together. They're gorgeous. So, I can schedule the meeting on Saturday if you allow us to meet your mom and have dinner or something."

"I'll see about that. Sometimes, my mom can't speak English."

"What language does she speak?"

"College professor language. She uses many large words, I can't make out what she is trying to say. Mom did well with Sigrid. She won't be up to it before Wednesday, so after that, I'll ask her to meet my friends."

"Is she going to meet Alpine?"

"I haven't spoken to him since the morning of the incident. I miss him so much, though. In a short time, he became my backbone. My conversations with him made my upside down world better and he made my heart smile without even knowing I had a situation."

"Why haven't you called him?"

"I had spoken to him early into the morning on the Wednesday and was to call him when I got off. So much had gone wrong at work and with you, I stopped to buy some alcohol. When I got home, there was holy terror. When I was able to talk, I didn't know what I would say."

"He didn't call you?"

"For a few days after I was able move, I called and left messages, but I got no return calls. I would rather never speak to him again than to be rejected."

"I think you should call again, Bonita. You will see him at all of the functions and the wedding. He told Koffer that he loved you and wanted to make you his wife."

"Really? I want to be his wife, too. That gives me hope. I pray this works out."

"I have to go to work in the morning. I love you, Bonita."

"I love you, Jaza and I am glad we are back together."

෬෭

Bonita's first night alone after the incident went well. All day Monday, she sat planning her life because she refused to let Bruce hold her hostage in his death. The dead part of her history was buried. She considered talking to her mom concerning her inheritance. Bonita decided to build a business. She hoped Jean would have a change of heart so that she could share with her and her family. *Jesus, I could not let Mom know I feel that way. I am stable enough in me to take control in every area. Like Janet Jackson, I'm in Control.*

It was about 3:30, her doorbell rang. When she opened the door, Kate jumped into her arms.

"Bonita, I am glad to hold you alive! I was scared. I thought you were going to die!"

"I am alive, you can breathe now. How are things at the Wisdom Well?"

"All of the patients miss you a lot. Mrs. Bowel Movement cries for you. She says no one gives her the senekot right to keep her bowels moving and as soon as you get back, she is going to tell on everybody."

"She is very funny, but if she doesn't stop, she is going to poop her brains out. I think she gets her ecstasy from those frequent bowel movements."

"What's that?"

"It's ok, Kate. Are you hungry? We can finish off the food from yesterday. The food was very good. I wonder if there is New Orleans food left. Eating that food put me in the mood for another brunch at Lloyd's home."

"We are going to finish it off at this meal setting. My mom comes tomorrow; I will save some of the food for her so that neither of us will have to cook."

"Your mom's coming tomorrow?"

"Yes, court is on Wednesday. Sigrid and my mom will be there. Don't cry Kate. My attorney says it is just a formality for me to be there. He has shared all of his findings with the DA and the DA shared his findings with my attorney. He is going to move for a dismissal of the case and the district attorney will agree."

"So, what does that mean?"

"Hopefully, it means that it will be thrown out."

"I want the best for you, Bonita. I am sober today because I could not let you down. I didn't want you to wake up and find me on the street. Your love for me is what gave me strength."

They had taken the food out of the refrigerator to warm and the doorbell rang. Bonita was then greeted by Carmen and Jaza.

"Yooo, we brought the party!" Carmen called out.

"Carmen, you are jazzing it up right," Kate saied.

Bonita looked on with a broad smile and said, "It is good to have my gang back."

Chapter 13

"ALL RISE. THE HONORABLE Judge George Neutrophulus presiding," the bailiff called out.

"Please take your seats," the judge said.

"State verses Bonita Advent," the bailiff said.

"How does the defendant plead?"

"Not guilty, sir," Bonita said.

"You are here to face charges of an either way offense. I will hear the testimony and decide if there is sufficient evidence to proceed. This is not a trial and there is no jury. Do you understand what I have said to you?"

"Yes, your honor."

"Do you agree to be tried here in this court?"

"Yes, your honor."

"State the charges."

"First count: Second Degree Murder, Second Count Manslaughter," the prosecutor said.

Judge Neutrophlus voice frightened Bonita and he said, "We shall proceed with the evidence."

"Your honor, if it please the court, I'd like to ask that the hearing be postponed for two weeks," Bonita's attorney said.

The Prosecutor agreed with the motion.

"We will hear evidence or move to Crown court," the judge said. "This is a murder case."

"Yes, your honor," my attorney stated in a weak voice. "We shall proceed."

The prosecutor interjected, "Your Honor, I would like to request 24 hours for my witnesses to arrive, as some are out of state."

"Is the suspect considered a risk?" the judge asked.

"No, your Honor we don't believe her to be a risk at this time. She and her counsel have been cooperative."

"Bail will be continued. Court will adjourn until I p.m. tomorrow."

Bonita's mother asked loudly, "What is going on? What happened?"

"Order will be maintained in the court," the judge said.

Sigrid took Bonita's mom from the courtroom.

"This came unexpected to me, Mrs. Advent," Bonita's attorney said to her.

"Please don't. Don't call me Mrs. Advent. Bonita is sufficient, thank you, sir. I didn't expect this either. What is going to happen now?"

"I knew there was a little chance that the judge would ask for more information about the case. I have prepared some, but I will need you to come to my office so that I can prepare you for tomorrow."

"Oh my God. Will I have to testify?"

"No one can tell your story of anguish better than you. It is your decision, but know that the prosecutor will not be nice once you take the stand. I must also say to you that Mrs. Garden has become witness for the state and a hostile witness for us."

"The prosecutor seems so nice. He agreed to stand with you on my behalf. You think he will be mean if I take the stand?"

"At that time, he didn't have Mrs. Garden. His job is to prove that you deliberately killed your husband. His feelings have nothing to do with it, so don't take it personally."

"Is there anything I can do to avoid this?"

"Take a plea. The D.A. offered you seven year of probation."

"What does that mean?"

"That means for seven years, you must sign in with your officer, pay your fines and your life will not be your own. "

"No, No. I will take my chances at the hearing. I don't want my mom present for that."

"Then tell her tonight. She will hear more in court tomorrow. It may sound better coming from you. The courtroom is open to the public and we cannot stop her from being there."

We walked out into the lobby where my mom and Sigrid were. Like a defensive mother bear, she ran to me and asked, "Bonita, what's going to happen to you? I am afraid. What do we do now?"

I held my crying mom in my arms and said, "It's all ok, Mom. The judge needs more information to prove that I am not guilty. I'll be through with this tomorrow. We are gonna be ok."

"Are you sure?"

"Mom, I promise, but I am going over to my attorney's office to prepare for tomorrow."

"I'll take her home and stay with her for tonight," Sigrid said.

"I will call you guys when I am ready"

"We will be waiting."

◌◌

My attorney appeared collected as we sat down at a table and chair to go over the events for the next day.

"Ms. Bonita, tell me about Mrs. Garden. What is your relationship with her?"

"She is Mr. Advent's mother."

"Mr. Advent, meaning the deceased?"

"Yes."

"Why does he call her Mrs. Garden and his name is Mr. Advent?"

"I am not sure. That subject was never entered into. His dad's last name, who is her husband, is Advent."

"Where did you meet this guy?"

"At their family's church."

"How long were you a member of the church before you started dating?"

"We never dated, it was nothing like that."

"Don't keep me pulling for answers."

"Ok, Mrs. Garden and my dad were best friends. I was nineteen years old when my dad was diagnosed with a terminal disease. My dad wanted to leave me with a man who he thought would take care of me, protect me and provide so that he could die in peace. Mrs. Garden told my dad that her son was a perfect candidate. She was ready for him to get out of her house. My dad went over to have a talk with him and was charmed out of his socks. Against my mom 's wishes, Dad had the wedding planned."

"What did your dad do when he started beating you?"

"He did not hit me when my dad was alive and that was five years after we were married."

"You two didn't have any children?"

"We did not have sex prior to my dad dying. We had separate bedrooms. Sometimes, I slept at my parents and he slept at his mom's. I would see his around, but the entire family was strange. I can't explain the situation."

"I need you to tell me about Mrs. Garden."

"Mrs. Garden is the church mother. She is the head lady in the church and she did everything Bruce told her to do. One day, when Bruce let me out of the closet, I went over to the church, sore and weak.

She looked at me and said, 'I know what you are going through and you have to get out of here.' That was about eight months after my dad died. She made arrangements for the church to give me the scholarship to nursing school. He did not interrupt my education because it was exposed to the church. Two months before I finished school, he beat me terribly. He told the church I was in an accident and told the hospital that I ran into a pole with my car. I was hospitalized for seven days. The school made arrangements for me to make up the work. He became furious because I was going to graduate. He accused me of adultery and I was afraid for my life at that time. He lost all self-control and he started following me around, hurting himself and reporting that me and my boyfriend did it. Mrs. Garden took him off for six days. He came back much better, but she told me that I need to make arrangements to leave before it gets worse. 'Leave town,' she said. I found this town. I did not speak to her again until she called me in the hospital to apologize for all I experienced with her son."

"Did you have sex with your husband? Was there romance in your marriage? Did you hate him?"

"I don't hate him because when I walked away, I left all the baggage. Bruce would jump me whenever he was physically abusive. I have never had romance from anyone."

"Bonita, the prosecutor is going to ask you questions and I am going to prepare you for that now. There are big holes in the Mrs. Garden's story. I am going to keep all my senses open with Mrs. Garden. The states also have a psychiatrist as a witness. Neither of us was able to subpoena any of the church members. I do have signed statement from two members, though."

"I didn't remember to tell you that Bruce has a son and he is the pastor of the church now. Well, he was before this happened."

"I have enough testimony concerning the son and everyone involved to get you set free today."

"You do? I have never met the son. It was Mrs. Garden who told me about him when she called me at the hospital."

"This mystery is growing. Mrs. Garden called you at the hospital?"

"Yes, to apologize for all that I had been through. She wanted me to know that he loved me and did not hold resentment. She hoped that I would be ok."

∽

Bonita saw the look of horror on her mom's face as approached the car.

"Mama, we are going to be alright. I am anxious. I want to cry. I am nervous and afraid, too, Mom. But, I know we will come out of this ok."

"Our girl will be fine," Sigrid told Bonita's mom.

"Mom, it will not be pretty in the courtroom tomorrow."

"What does that mean?"

"That means that I have gone through a lot and ugly things will be told. Do you think you can handle this?"

"If you went through it, I can listen to it. I love you, Bonita. You are all I have and without you, I have no reason to live."

"I will not respond to that now, Mom."

Bonita's thoughts of the future kept her from sleeping well. When she shut her eyes, she could see the ax going into his head. She wished she could turn back the hands of time. If she didn't go to jail when she was finished with court, she decided that she would not think about this again. She knew that she didn't directly kill him. It was an uncontrolled event. *What did I think would happen if I threw the ax? If he had gotten it, I would have been dead. Jesus, what was I thinking?*

It takes one mere event to change the course of life and draw all of the skeletons from the bottom of the closet where all the secrets are buried. Only a scavenger would dig graves. That man married her and he had an ex-wife and a son. Bonita couldn't stop her mind from thinking about it all.

Bonita realized that adulthood came with a big price. She understood that this was the place where she lost her innocence. She had been raped of her pride, dignity and confidence. She refused to lie to anyone and be robbed of the life she'd worked hard to find. Her mom wasn't upset when Bonita told her of her plan to not accept a plea. Her mom told her that she was willing to hear the ugliness that had occurred. She said it was actually good that she had to go through this because now, she could say that she was a woman. At that moment, Bonita wished she could cuddle under her dad's protection.

"We are going to do fine, ladies. In a few hours, all of this will be behind us never to speak of again," Sigrid said, as they drove to court the next morning.

Chapter 14

*A*S THEY ENTERED THE courtroom, there were people Bonita had not seen since she left home. Mrs. Garden gave her a big hug and said, "I love you and miss you so much."

Bonita's attorney came over to separate them and firmly exclaimed, "My client cannot have any contact with the witness."

When we arrived to our seats, he whispered, "Bonita, there is something about that woman that I do not trust. I vow to you that I will find the missing link to her."

"If it will help me, go get it."

The bailiff suddenly called out, "Court will come to order. All rise! The honorable Judge George Neutropholus presiding. All may be seated."

"The state calls Dr. William Pedix."

Dr. Pedix appeared calm as he took the stand and was sworn in. He was the expert psychiatrist witness who treated Bruce since he was 21. Bruce had been diagnosed with delusional jealousy, bipolar disorder and paranoia and should have been on medicine for years. The psychiatrist testified that his treatment was periodical because he could not convince his mother that only consistent treatment would help her son. He also testified that since Bruce's last exacerbation and hospitalization three years ago, he had been functioning with control in everyday life. After the psychiatrist's testimony was completed, Bonita realized that everyone in the court room felt sorry for the poor, sick man. *Judge, please don't fall for it. He is not innocent,* she thought. She had butterflies in her stomach and she felt like she was about to throw up.

Witnesses began coming in, one by one, each attempting to beat her soul into submission, but her heart wouldn't give out. Not this time. Today, her mom had taken her father's place by protecting her from the world. She knew her prayer to protect her.

Lloyd took the stand and the prosecutor's plan backfired on him. Lloyd testified that Bonita was on the other side of the room when he kicked the door in. He said that he saw the ax flying across the room into Bruce's head when he opened the door. What appeared to steal the hearts of the people in the room was his description of my appearance, how my face and my head were swollen and bruised beyond recognition.

Poor Kate, Bonita thought, as Kate cried on her way up to the witness stand. The tears didn't stop when the questions started and she ended up being considered a hostile witness. However, everything she had to say corroborated the testimony of the neighbors. Bonita didn't realize that her neighbors paid attention to her and she had no idea that they called the police twice that weekend.

Deacon Smith, Bruce's lifetime friend, took the testified that Bruce was a great humanitarian. According to him, his life had been spent loving and serving others.

Lord, don't let him fall dead from the seat from which he sits, please, Lord. This man saved my life twice by stepping in to stop Bruce from killing me.

He continued to go on with the Bruce fantasy. Bonita wrote to her attorney, 'These are all lies, stop him, object'. My attorney wrote back, 'We have bigger fish to fry. We don't want to seem petty to the court. We will recall as our witness if it is needed.' He was focused on Mrs. Garden and would not do anything else. Bonita felt desperate. She wrote back to him, 'I want to testify.'

Bruce's physician took the stand, but Bonita's medical report spoke for itself. He took longer than forty-five minutes answering questions about our conditions. Only fifteen of those minutes were used to describe the facial and cranial swelling, the fluid collection on my brain, severe weakness and periods of unconsciousness for days. And his final statement was that it was caused by trauma and blunt blows to the head.

Next was Bonita's turn. She was afraid and she could feel myself shaking as she was sworn in and took the stand. The answers to her attorney's questions were fluent and she began to feel confident. Then, suddenly, she was caught off guard by the prosecutor, who began tearing her apart. She wanted to get off the stand.

"Had Mr. Advent ever harmed or threatened you in the past?"

"Yes."

"Can you tell the court briefly of an incident where you were hurt?"

"After the church picnic about six months after my dad died, one of the brothers approached me and began to tell me that he thought I was wonderful and beautiful. He said that I encouraged the women and he went on with accolades. My husband became upset and firmly took me away. When we got in the car and drove off, he began to slap my face. When we arrived home, he began to beat me with a bat. Deacon Smith followed us into our home, pulled Bruce off of me , and he hit Bruce and said, 'Stop man. Stop before you do it again.' I was afraid to stay in our home, so he took me to a motel and paid for it. He told me to stay there until he came back for me and that I could not be with Bruce at this time."

"Did you report this incident to the police?"

"No, I didn't."

"Was this the only alleged incident of violence toward you?"

"No."

"There is not record of any domestic violence reported against Mr. Advent. Why didn't you go for help?"

"I was afraid he would kill me if I told," she said, shivering throughout her testimony.

"On the day of the incident, were you in fear of dying or receiving great bodily harm?"

"Yes, he kept hitting me and he began strangling me. He hit me with objects from the kitchen, like pots, cooking spoon and the chair."

"Usually the kitchen has sharp objects. Did he try to stab you or attempt to kill or seriously hurt you with a sharp object?"

"No he didn't. He laughed until I hit him with the glass pitcher. Then, he became angry."

"Mrs. Advent, was it a custom for you and your husband to fight often?"

"No, I never fought back; I would let him beat me so that it would be over quickly."

Bonita saw the tears falling from her mother's face and she saw a pain that she had never seen before. Bonita quickly decided to not talk about being starved and stuffed in the closet.

"Mrs. Advent, you had been in the house with your husband for three days. Did you have sex?"

"I wouldn't call it sex."

"Did your husband put his penis into your vagina?"

"Yes, but I..."

"Answer only the questions asked, please."

"I object," Bonita's attorney called out.

"Overruled," the judge said and directed the prosecution to proceed"

"You were in the house for four days . Did you try to leave?"

"Yes, but he said no Did you physically try to leave the house?"

"No, I was afraid he would get mad and hurt me."

"Mrs. Advent, was the danger real and imminent? You were there for four days in total. You did not fight for three of those days. Was the danger real and imminent?"

Bonita sat on the stand with tears streaming down her face. She could not think any longer and the judge's harsh voice brought her back to reality."Answer the question, Mrs. Advent."

"Yes, I think so. I believe... YES!" she answered, crying.

She could feel the prosecutor's aggression start to increase.

"Mrs. Advent, you were in the house four days with your husband whom you testified abused you. Only you knew the ax was under the chair in the living room and you have testified that that is where you spent most of the three days. You also testified that he slept in the living room. You never thought of escaping with the ax while he was asleep?"

Still crying, she shouted, "NO! NO!" Trying to compose herself did not work. The more she thought and looked at her mom, the more she felt like she was falling apart.

"What was your intention when you threw the ax?"

"I don't know, I don't know why I threw the ax."

He asked angrily, "What did you want to happen when you threw THAT ax?"

"I don't know!"

"Mrs. Advent, one last question" he said, as he leaned in toward me, "Remember you are under oath. Was there anything you could have done to protect yourself other than what you did?"

Bonita cried and shook her head. Her attorney stood and asked, "Could the record reflect that my client is shaking her head to denote no?"

The judge nodded and repeated, "Let the record reflect the defendant is shaking her head no."

"No further questions, your honor."

Her attorney assisted her in getting to seat and wiped her face.

The judge stated, "We will take a thirty minute recess."

Her attorney rushed her out to a back room. "It is ok, and we will be alright, Bonita. The hearing is not over yet."

Back into the courtroom, her attorney called the last witness, the dreaded Mrs. Garden, who refused to be sworn in because of her religious beliefs.

"Mrs. Garden, be sworn in or be charged with contempt of court. Will you raise your right hand?"

She finally agreed and after being sworn in, she slowly took the stand, turned, took a deep breath and sat down.

"Do you recognize this person?" Bonita's attorney asked, pointing at her.

When she nodded yes, he asked, "How did your meet her?"

"I was friends with her beloved father and I met her when he brought her to my home to become engaged with my son. He father was dear to me and he needed a husband for his daughter before he died."

"What was your relationship with Bonita?"

"I love her as if she was my own daughter. I arranged for the church to give her a scholarship to nursing school. It hurt my heart when she left us aftershe finished school without a word or warning. She did not make any effort to repay the tuition."

"Did Bonita understand that it was a loan the church had given her?"

"She came to us nineteen years old with only a high school education. We tried to help her."

"I'll rephrase my earlier question. Please define the relationship between you and Bonita. Did you get along? How did you two treat each other?"

"We cooked together. Bonita was at my home often. She was always respectful. Her mom was not present in her life, so I stepped into her place. We cooked together, shopped together and I mentored Bonita."

Bonita heard her mom coughing behind her and she thought she was going to pass out from the lies.

"Your honor, may I have a short recess?" her attorney asked.

"Five minute recess."

Her attorney escorted Bonita to the room behind the witness stand.

"Bonita, this woman's façade took me off guard. I have never seen anything like it. We both know that she is lying. More than that, I know that you love her and what she is doing on the witness stand hurts your heart. Keep in mind that there is no debt a mother won't go through for her child. Trust me, Bonita. She can't hurt you anymore. I have enough evidence and another witness, if necessary, who will come here today. We will end this atrocity. Is your mom ok?"

"I'm ok and my mom is stronger than I ever thought."

"Can I see you smile?"

Bonita smiled and gave him a big hug.

The court reconvened and the court was called to order. The judge reminded Mrs. Garden that she was under oath.

"Mrs. Garden, you have described the relationship you had with Bonita. Is that correct?"

"Yes it is."

"And how long had you known her dad?"

"We had been friends since we were thirteen years old."

"Did you have mutual friends? Did you know both his wife and mistress?"

"I knew his wife and I knew about Bonita's mother. We do have common friends. I don't hang around much because I have a different lifestyle."

"Then you were aware that Bonita was a product of an adulterous relationship with her mom whom you had not met because you didn't approve of, yet you sacrificed your son. Had your son previously been married?"

Mrs. Garden hesitated and said, "I'm sorry I don't understand the question."

"Let me rephrase. Did your son stand before your God and man to make a covenant with a woman prior to meeting Bonita?"

Mrs. Garden didn't answer the question and the attorney went on with the next question.

"Bruce Advent, Jr. Who were his parents and who raised him?"

"My husband adopted him and raised him as his own."

"Your husband? Are you and your husband estranged?"

"Yes, we are divorced and he remarried. He is the pastor of a church 200 miles away."

"Your church is his family church, correct?"

"It is not my church, but yes sir. The church was built by my husband's family. When we divorced, my son became the pastor to keep the church history of the Advent family. And now, his grandson, Bruce David Advent III, is pastor."

"I will go back to a previous question. Who is little Bruce's mother? Who is his father?"

Mrs. Garden stumbled and said, "My deceased son."

"Who is his mother?"

She gaped and stared like a deer caught in headlights.

"We will come back to that question. Were you aware of the occurrence of domestic violence in your son's marriage to Bonita and if so, when did it happen?"

"I did notice that Bonita's demeanor changed after her father died. I did speak with her in attempts to help her through her grieving process."

"Let me go back to my previous question. Who is Little Bruce's mother?"

Mrs. Garden turned to the Judge and asked, "Do I have to answer this question?"

The judge turned to the attorney and asked, "Does this line of questioning have relevance to this case."

"It is strongly related to root of this case, your honor."

"Answered the question," he ordered.

"His mother's name is Jane Clairmonte."

"Isn't his mother's name is indeed Jane Clairmonte Advent and where is she today?"

"She is in a nursing home in the town where my husband lives. She is disabled and doesn't walk or speak."

"What would put a young woman in that physical state? Remember, you are under oath."

"She was beaten."

Mrs. Garden looked uncomfortable. She fidgeted in her seat. Before Bonita's attorney could ask another question, she said, "She was beaten by my son. She was pregnant and he found she had been with another guy and the baby was not his."

"Was the couple married, Mrs. Garden?"

"Yes," she cried out, shaking her head. "They were married!"

"Was she pregnant at the time he beat her near death?"

"Objection, your honor," the prosecutor yelled out. "The court has not determined that he beat her to near death."

"Sustained. Do not let the record reflect the last question. Proceed."

"How long after the incident in question was the baby born?"

"She was eight months pregnant and the baby was delivered that night."

"How did your husband come to raise your grandson, little Bruce?"

"He decided to leave our family," she said, angrily. "He wanted to leave us and take care of Jane and the baby."

"He was the pastor in the town where you're lived. His family built and nourished the church for four generations and he left his young son to be the pastor."

"He wanted my baby to go to jail! He left me to go take care of another woman and her child. He left –"

"Mrs. Garden, how did you know that your son had begun physically abusing my client?"

"I saw that look in her eyes. It was very familiar to me." Mrs. Garden mind seemed to have wandered. "I saw the look of a beaten, raped woman in her eyes. She could not look me in the eyes anymore."

"The look was familiar, to whom was it familiar with, Mrs. Garden?" he asked, gently."

"Myself," she cried. "It reminded me of the look I had in eyes when..." She fell silent.

"When? Can you complete the statement?"

Mrs. Garden did not answer and Bonita's attorney went on to another question.

"Why did your son call you Mrs. Garden and not mother? That is unusual. Your married name is Advent and your maiden name is Smith."

Mrs. Garden sat whimpering and the judge said, "Answer the question."

"Because he wanted to dismiss the maternal strings." She became anxious, angry and out of control. "Can I leave now, Judge? I can't take this." She pushed to the front of the seat. "Can I leave?"

"The look you saw in Bonita's and your own eyes, did you see that look in Jane's eyes before he married her?

Before the DA could complete an objection, Mrs. Garden said, "He forced my baby to marry Jane."

"Did you see that look in her eyes?"

"Her parents said my baby raped her and she was found to be pregnant three months later. They forced him to marry her. My baby couldn't go to prison."

"Did your son have a problem raping women, Mrs. Garden? How many women did your baby rape? Whose look was familiar? Who, Mrs. Garden?"

"Me!" she screamed. "He raped me! Are you satisfied?! That's why I had him marry Bonita! Because I couldn't take it anymore. He raped and beat me. He was sick. He needed a wife."

The emotion in the courtroom was buzzing. Bonita's attorney was quiet for a moment.

"Is that why you warned Bonita to go to school and get out?"

"I knew he was coming to that point. I had mixed feelings. I wanted her to get out safely, but I did not want to go back to that same hell. I knew that if I mentioned nursing in front of the church, that would keep her safe a little while longer and if the church knew, he would give us a break."

"Give us a break. Did he abuse you while married to Bonita?"

"He was sick, don't you understand?"

"Is violence a part of his diagnosis?"

"Why are you making me say all these things about my baby? He was a good boy and it was wrong for him to die like a dog!"

"Why didn't you seek more help for your son instead of aiding him? He was sick and the medicine ruined his life."

"Shut up! Shut up!" Mrs. Garden screamed in rage. "I hate you, Advent! You just want to hurt my baby. You love everyone but him!" Mrs. Garden looked around the courtroom, confused.

"One more question, if I may your honor"

"Proceed with one more if you must."

"Mrs. Garden, did you know that your son had found Bonita and was going after her?"

147

"He didn't plan to hurt her. He said he was going to bring her back. She is his wife. She should have been there for him. I was tired, don't you understand that? She should have come back. She knew how he gets. She must have made him... "

"No further questions," he said, angrily.

"You may step down," the bailiff said. "You are not to leave this building until further instructions."

Despite all of the lies she said, Bonita's heart went out to her. There was no one there to support her. She hoped the Deacon Smith would help her.

Mrs. Garden stopped when she was walking past Bonita and she said, "I am sorry..."

Before she could complete her statement, Bonita's mother stood angrily and said, "Don't talk to my baby. I pray you go to hell from the church pulpit you speak from."

"Quiet! There will be no further outbursts in this courtroom. We will break for a thirty-minute recess."

The courtroom felt cold, numb and quiet to Bonita. The only thing she could hear was Mrs. Garden crying.

The Judge returned in less than thirty minutes and the bailiff instructed her to stand and her attorney did, as well.

"The court finds the charges against you unsustainable," the judge said. "You are acquitted."

Bonita turned around, crying and she hugged her attorney before walking out of the courtroom.

"Bonita, do you want to stay and find out what happens to Mrs. Garden?" he asked her.

"I really want to leave Mrs. Garden and all of that life behind, right now. A big part of me feels sorry for her."

The four of them, Bonita, her mother, her attorney and Kate walked out of the courtroom to the car.

"I can't believe this stuff is real," Bonita murmured.

"Believe it, Bonita," my attorney said. "I did meet with Mr. Advent, the daddy. He told me all of the information that was exposed today in court and more. He did not know if Mrs. Advent-Garden was having sex with her son when he was younger. She did have an abortion when he was fifteen. I am not sure if his illness did not stem from his mother's illness, but she refused treatment for herself. I won't tell you anymore of the gruesome details. You know enough to be free.

Chapter 15

*T*HIS IS A LONG *road coming to myself, Lord Jesus. Every time I come to the point where I think I have it all, a meteor storm comes and turns all of the pieces of my life into particles of dust, putting new, unfamiliar planets in my orbit. I pray this is the end. It has to be the bottom of my pit; I can only go up from here.*

In a strange way, she felt good about all that had happened. In this midst of it all, she felt like she had found herself.. She had a saving grace from the beginning of it all – her mom and her inheritance from her father. She did not reach for it because she would not have known about her strength, nor my mother's. All she needed was the Lord. It was a painful process, pulling strength from the bowels of her spirit and soul. But, she found the weapons of warfare that she needed to strategize for the victory of life. Pain had become her partner in war. All of the battles are not won, but she considered herself a conqueror.

The drive home with her mom and Sigrid was a quiet one. Sigrid did not go into work because court was overwhelming and she was exhausted. Most of all, though, Mr. Emmanuel missed her much.

Sigrid had been support for both Bonita and her mom. There were times through this ordeal, especially during the trial, that Sigrid had been their lifeline. They could not breathe or eat. Sigrid reminded Bonita of the old days when the community was the family.

Bonita and mother lay in bed for the entirety of that evening. They cried talked and drew life from one another. Bonita got to know and build a relationship with her mother. She knew her mother hated Mrs. Garden, but she had no idea how much. Her mom called her a liar and a manipulator who always had her life in the gutter until Bonita's dad convinced her to marry Reverend Advent. That was when the reverend and her dad broke off their friendship because his life went to hell. Bonita's mom said that woman had been crazy for a long time and for some reason, her father felt responsible for her. Her mom called Bruce the son and said that she thought him to be strange, but not as crazy as his mom. They had never met. Reflecting on how much she loved and honored Bonita's dad, her mom thought Bonita viewed him as a god. She waited for Bonita to protest marrying Bruce and how it would have not been a wedding.

"I would have done anything my dad thought was good for me because I knew how much he loved me. He would say to me often how no one in the world loved me like he did. Thinking of those moments, I can feel his kiss and it makes his love for me tangible today. I love you daddy."

They were both quiet for a moment before Bonita spoke again.

"Why would God allow such things to go on, especially in his church?" she asked.

Bonita didn't know if her mom was close to God, but she was surprised as she imparted a lot of wisdom.

"God didn't allow any of that, Bonita. What makes us human is our freedom in Him. Our free will is a gift that most of us abuse. We have the right to choose and he will not override man's choices, good or bad. But, he will interrupt the bad when it will harm the people who choose to do his good."

"I am finished with church and God," Bonita said. "I don't know what was happening to me and I loved Him and talked good to others about Him all the time. But, I think God should have rescued me before all of this happened."

"Baby, God is God all by himself. Sometimes, people are caught up in religion and church and the Lord gets blocked out. The problem is we don't know our God as well as the enemy does. And secondly, much of what people say comes from God is not Him; it's the flesh trying to get glory before Him. Flesh and wrong can never be right. We are victorious only through the blood of Jesus. The devil knows that and he gets most of us with the big okey doke through a camouflage of lies and making it all shine like gold. I am not trying to tell you what to believe, nor am I telling you what to do. The truth is as simple as just asking for it.

The two held each other until they fell asleep.

When Bonita woke up the next morning, she found her mom awake and preparing breakfast. The house smelled like it did in the mornings when she was twelve.

"We have to get a good man conversation started over breakfast," Bonita's mom said.

"How will I know if he is a good man?" Bonita asked.

Her mom motioned for her to lean in closer to listen to what she was about to say. "You know he is the man for you if he treats you like God does. God created man to love, protect, cover and provide. If he is not doing that, he is not your man."

"Mom, break it down in real language, please."

"Are you a big girl?"

"Oh Lord. Well, if I am not a big girl now, I will be when you finish with me."

"He will make sure you have a place to sleep. If it is a shack in the winter, it would be full of blankets to keep you warm. He will always take your case, wrong or right. He will take care of transportation. If it's a car, he will take care of it. If it is a bus, he will always be at the bus stop. And in the bed, he doesn't turn over until you are finished and satisfied. Sometimes, it might take a lick and a stick."

"I don't want to think about all that. But, what I did experience with Dad and Alpine is that the man for you will keep a smile on your face and you will smile whenever you think of them. I miss Dad and I miss Alpine. I will call Alpine when I get a moment today. He always makes everything feel better."

Bonita was quiet for a moment, lost in thought.

"What are you thinking about, baby?"

"Daydreaming about Alpine. But, Mom, I have something we must talk about. I was at the fantasy party. Do you know what that is?"

"Yes, I do."

"Oh my God, don't say no more about it. I did not know what a climax was in the fantasy party. When I blurted it out, everyone looked at me as if I was from Mars. I felt like an idiot."

"You didn't climax when you were married, Bonita?"

"Mom, I don't want to talk about that."

"Have you had a climaxed since the fantasy party?"

"The girls brought me a dildo and magic lips."

"I can tell you didn't use it. You really don't have to have vaginal stimulation to have a climax, but a penis in your vagina makes it better."

"Aw, Mom," Bonita groaned.

"A climax is a high point of excitement that causes contractions in your vagina. It produces ecstasy and beyond. If you get it right, there are not words to describe it. There are not that many bad boys around."

"Mom! The closest thing I had to sex when I was married was times he would pin me down and force himself in me. And then, he was raging mad."

Her mom got up from the table and held Bonita tight in her arms. "Baby, I am sorry that I allowed your father to keep you in a box. I am going to pray that God heels your heart."

"I have met someone who makes me smile and makes everything right, especially when I feel at my worst."

"I was wondering when you were going to tell me about him. Do you smile when you think about him? I see a great big blush. This might be him."

"He makes my body tingle when he pulls me close to him."

"You may be close to experiencing a climax. What about when you kiss him?"

"We never kissed"

"Poor baby. You are your father's child. How did he take you going through all of this?"

"I haven't spoken to him about it. I will call him when I am alone."

"If the relationship is new, I think you did it the best way. Do you think you will be ok from here? If so, I am going to go home today. I have purchased a ticket for you to come up to see me. You don't have to stay here lonely. Just come to Mom and she will help you heal."

"Mama, I love you."

"I love you more, Bonita, but I have a mister who misses me and is ready for me to come home. At home, I can take care of both of you."

"I'll be ok until I get back to you. Is he married, Mom?"

"Don't ask if you don't want to know. But, not technically."

"Mom, I want you to have your own husband. You are telling me about God and look what you do."

"Doesn't matter what I do. God is still God. I am not big enough to change who He is. He is the almighty eternal God."

"Mom, you are going to end up lonely and alone."

"That reminds me, when your dad died, he left you an inheritance. My bank account is overloaded and I need you to come and get your money."

"Alright. No more to be said."

"I am not lonely. He is there whenever I need and want him."

"I remember. So was daddy."

∾

After dropping her mom off at the airport, Bonita rushed home to call Alpine. He did not sound at all like himself. She expected her world to take off like a rocket ship, but it crashed from obit and set her life on fire. Her heart fell apart when she heard the disgust in voice when he realized it was me.

"What do you want?" he asked.

Bonita felt crushed. He called her a murdering liar. He said that she had tried to trick him into sin and that he knew that she was married. There was such venom in his voice that Bonita was taken aback. He said that she had gotten him involved in her garbage, but the part that took her breath away was when he said that he knew that he would never trust a desperate, game-playing female from the Internet again.

"How dare you even call my phone?"

He went on and on until Bonita finally meekly hung up the phone. After that, she lay in bed in a catatonic state for two days, speaking only to her mother when she called.

Jaza arrived at Bonita's to go out shopping for her Maid of Honor dress. Bonita opened the door and immediately started sobbing.

"Oh my God, Bonita, What's wrong?" Jaza asked, as she began crying, as well.

"Jaza, I have fallen in love with Alpine. But, he refuses to speak to me ever again. I have to get over him."

156

Jaza was not surprised and she held her in her arms. "We will get past this, Bonita. Will it be too much for you to be in my wedding?"

"Three strikes, you're out, Jaza."

"I asked because you will have to walk with him in the wedding. He is the best man."

"I don't think he will do it, Jaza."

"Koffer told him you were the Maid of Honor."

"What did he say?"

"He wanted me to remove you from the position and I said that that was appalling and not a consideration. He can walk with you or change his position. He said he and Koffer have been friends since he moved here from Germany and would not consider relinquishing his position of honor. Alpine agreed to walk with you for the wedding. It was only a vow of agreement to our commitment."

Tears began to fall from Bonita' eyes again and she struggled to hold herself together.

"Let me help you get dressed. Wear something beautiful; you will feel better. Let's hurry. We have got to go."

Once she was dressed, Bonita and Jaza headed out.

"We will go to eat first," Bonita said. "I want to get over these emotions before I go into the bridal shop. I can't make Alpine understand that though I was married, my heart wasn't married."

"I believe that, Bonita. I would have never guessed you had a man before. It did not show at all."

"Alpine is the first guy I wanted to share my life with and am willing to make the necessary changes to have him for a lifetime."

Chapter 16

*T*HE FAMILY TOOK CENTER seat for the bridal shower. They were not exactly excited that Bonita was the Maid of Honor. Jaza's mom thought it should have been her sister, Susie. Koffer's family looked at them all as though they were peasants. Bonita had a quiver deep in the pit of her stomach because she didn't know if Alpine had told them that she was a murderer.

"Your colors for your wedding are beautiful," Bonita said. "Cranberry, chocolate and a hint of cream and gold trim. Well done."

"My mom is working on my nerves," Jaza moaned. "She is trying to take over and she has no clue of the planning arrangements. She has to stop before I lose it, Bonita."

"Jaza, I don't remember you telling me your mom was coming. What –"

"Have a conversation with her and you will understand why I didn't tell her about the wedding at the last minute."

"Maybe I will go over to have a talk with her."

"Please, don't!"

"Ok, ok. What do you need me to do?"

"Can you pick up my dress?"

"You want me to do that now?"

"No, dummy. Tomorrow morning. I have to have breakfast with my new in-laws. Look at them, looking over this place like 'What is my son doing'?"

"His mom reminds me of Queen Elizabeth," Bonita said, chuckling.

"You wrong for that one!"

"Ok, peasant. Isn't that what the prince of England's wife is called?

Both girls laughed. "Who gives a damn," Jaza said. "Their son is taking good care of me."

"God does answer prayers," Bonita said, hugging her. Just then, Koffer called Jaza over to meet his uncle.

"You must be Bonita," Jaza's mom said.

"Yes ma'am, I am. How are you?"

"What part do have you to play in this?"

"I am sorry, ma'am, I –"

"You think I am stupid, don't you?"

"Oh, not at all, ma'am. I am sorry for anything I've said or done that would give you such an impression." Jaza's mom stood firm with her hands on her hips, but Bonita saw hurt in her eyes that weakened her heart. "I don't know how to answer your question. My position in the wedding is –"

"I know what your position is. Undeserved. Did you know that Jaza has a sister?"

"Yes ma'am, I do. Jaza and I have been through a lot, though."

"'Through' is your mother raising you and your sister alone until you thought you were grown at eighteen and left home. Treating me like I'm trash and allowing total strangers to do your wedding. That's your mama's job."

Bonita allowed her to vent because it seemed to be therapeutic for her heart.

"She has this so fancy and she knows I can't afford any of this stuff. I guess you helped pay for all of this. She told me you are her boss. She is just trying to embarrass me."

"Ma'am, I did not pay for anything. Do you see Koffer's mother sitting over there?"

"Who does she think she is? She helped pay for this, too." Mama had tears in her eyes."

"Did you know that your daughter risked everything to find a rich man to take care of her. His parents could have put on this show. This man, Koffer, did all of this to give your daughter the wedding of her dreams. He gave her the money and she hired a planner and she told us where to be."

Bonita saw some relief in her eyes. "How did you get to be maid of honor? Is she ashamed of us?"

"Ashamed? You are all she talks about. You will have to speak at gift time tomorrow." Bonita was preparing her because she knew that Koffer's parents had bought them a trip on the French Rivera, one of Koffer's desires.

"That's the shit I'm talking about," she said, becoming fired up again. "It took everything I had to get to this damn wedding."

Susie came over and saw her mom was upset. She stepped in front of Bonita and asked, "Mama, what's wrong? What is she saying to you?"

"I am saying that your mama is the greatest gift ever to Koffer and your sister. She brought you girls up alone with no help. Koffer, with all of his money, could not find what his life needed until he found Jaza. You guys are staying in the guest hotel that has been prepared for you?"

"What?" Mama said. "They think we are too poor..."

"Mama," Susie said, putting her finger up. "What hotel?"

"Here, there are rooms assigned for your family. We will have to get Bonita to tell us how many rooms you all have."

"We've already checked in."

"After the shower has ended, go cancel and get your money back. Before you leave here, check into your rooms. You all will have a great time," Bonita assured them.

It ended up being a marvelous evening after the champagne was flowing. Everyone dropped their inhibitions and they became one big family. Bonita drank only water because the bachelorette party was that night and she had to be ready. The games were funny and the night ended up being a blast.

Chapter 17

"_H_ELLO, BONITA."

"Yes, good morning, bride."

"I don't know how I let you talk me into allowing my mom to come with us to pick up my dress."

"The bachelorette party is tonight. You can drink your joy back into existence," she said. All the girls chuckled. "I think that would be a marvelous moment and more special if I was not there. This will be the bridge that your relationship needs to bring healing."

"Ok, I'll accept the psychology. Hell no. I am here to pick you up and you are coming. Last night, my mom and I hugged. I don't think that has happened since I was eight years old. After we talked, I realize that she always thought I felt like she wasn't good enough and I always thought she hated me."

"What could have caused that?"

"My dad walked out when my sister and I were young. Well, he didn't really leave; he just stayed drunk all the time, alcoholic. We walked around as if he was not there, like he was nonexistent. I was always a child who wanted more. I knew I would be rich one day."

They all laughed again. "My dad would say I had a rich mind and a poor behind. Mom says that was stressful for her because she was providing all she could. She treated me like I was stressing her and I took it as hate. We never discussed our feelings until last night. So, thank you, Bonita."

"For what?"

"For being the stone breaker for my family. I spoke with my dad last night and told him that I wished he was here; I hadn't spoken to him in years. This week has been a week of restoration and growth. We are enjoying one another like a real family."

"That makes me happy, also. I should have invited my mother. She would have enjoyed the wedding."

"Why didn't you?"

"Because I would have been uncomfortable. I would have spent the week trying to hide how much I love Alpine and hide my heartbreak. Just too much."

"How would your mom have known that, Bonita?"

"Moms have a way of knowing. I did tell her that I had met him and we both thought he would be the one. My mom knows me well. He spoke to me last night."

"He did? What did he say?"

"He asked how I was and he hoped that I felt better, etc. etc."

"What did you say?"

"I responded. I told him I was doing well, absolutely wonderful."

"He made sure I saw him," Jaza said. "He smiled at me from the corner of his face and then, he deliberately avoided making eye contact for the remainder of the night."

"I missed the dance. I was sure he would have asked me to dance."

"No silly, I —"

"I am turned on when I see him," Bonita confessed. "After the wedding, I am going to spend two weeks with my mom."

"Two weeks? The old people at the home miss you."

"I miss them, too. But this last little piece of me I have to fix so that I can go on. It is what is best for them, Mom and me."

"I have faith in you, Bonita. You will do just fine."

Susie and Bonita climbed in the back while Mama sat in the passenger side. Jaza's mom seemed to be more cheerful than both of her daughters had seen her in years. Mama began telling the story of her wedding day with her husband and the love that permeated from recapturing the moment. The story was breathtaking to Bonita. Jaza became emotional and asked her mother what had happened and her mother became sad. She began to explain that the town's plant closed and her husband had been put out of work.

"Grandpa Jimmy came to our house constantly to degrade and emasculate him. He started by getting very drunk on days Grandpa Jimmy would come over and eventually, he took himself into another world."

Mama looked visibly upset and it was obviously because he had taken her love away. She said how she hated Grandpa Jimmy.

They all walked quietly into the bridal store. Bonita imagined that they were all reminiscing on the love they missed. The enchanted beauty of Jaza's Cinderella fantasy dress that only a fairy Godmother could deliver caused all the women to become more emotional. Jaza's mom said she would not trade that moment for the world and she had to be present when her daughter adorned that dress. Jaza vowed that it would be their personal moment and that her mom would ride with her to the wedding. Mama got a new dress that complemented the bride's dress and Susie and Bonita got everything they were missing to make their wedding attire complete. Then, they dropped Mama off with the wedding dress.

All of the girls went over to Bonita's house to prepare for the bachelorette party. Of course, everyone had to comment on Bonita's tight chocolate jeans with rhinestones and maid of honor t-shirt with stones and sequins. They thought she was hot, but Bonita thought she looked like the wedding Christmas tree.

They rode to the club Durgesa had chosen and surprisingly, the same sex drinks she had served at the fantasy party were being served that night. Bonita found out later that she did supply the penis straws and all of the sex paraphernalia of the night. And the party began. All of the girls got in a circle, singing the shot song and guzzling down Patron shots. Bonita was the counter because the Patron was like narcotics to her system; she just couldn't handle it. After the shots, they all got on the mechanical bull. Bonita was the only person able to stay on the bull, as she only had her green apple martinis. The girls were tying their shirts above the belly button and beating the bull with whips. Bonita looked on and smiled, thinking that after all the Patron, the girls had entered another world.

When they did finally sit at the table, banana splits were prepared. *All the girls are going to throw up, for sure*, Bonita thought to herself. The sex dice started to roll. Bonita was relieved when her dice rolled 'lick it' and she and everyone else laughed when the bride had to 'rub it' and Kate had to 'suck it'. But Susie was the winner; it was amazing to see her 'nipple it'.

The party went well into the night and the girls had drank more than a distillery can produce in a days' time. Suddenly, Durgesa announced the last surprise for the girls, the infamous Mr. Incredible. The room fell silent as a big, fine, muscular hunk danced around the room. Bonita felt something in private places on her body that made her want to jump on him. He played towards her, but she ran and held on to the table for dear life. He moved on and apparently did not want to waste his time on a scaredy cat. The bride was happy when he lifted her up in the air and sat her on his face and he had her begging for more. Bonita's nipples were hard and she wished she had let him sit her on his face. The girls were fired up and he was the best entertainment Bonita had seen at any party. In the end, she understood why they called him Mr. Incredible.

Chapter 18

*W*HEN YOU SPEAK TO me, your words melt into the heart of my soul
 And they are like a fresh wind, enlightening my spirit.
Your move is smooth
Like a gazelle springing across wild acreage
Like an antelope, roaming the planes.
You maneuver in my spirit, gazing across my future.
It is me and you.
Bounce on me, my love.
Rein in my heart, my majestic one.
Deny all nature and rain into my flesh.

Let my spirit meet your spirit and my soulmeet your soul.
I wait anxiously for your touch in my dreams.
My days are paved with thoughts of you.
Your tender kiss takes my breath away.
Our love is the energy that ignites my days.
Your laughter is the fuel that pushes me into our future.

Holding hands with you is so divine.
We, together, make the perfect DNA.

Ooh, you are awesome!
I know that your love for me is a gift from God.
You bring 100% to this relationship.
You don't think twice to give your life to me.
Every day, I try to love you more.
My moments are not without thoughts of you.
My heart pounds at my amazing thoughts.
Living out God's plan is so easy with you.
I know our love, our unity, is eternal.
Thank you for your love.

"This is a perfect fall day for my friend's wedding," Bonita said to Jaza's sister standing next to her. "The cool, colorful leaves on the trees provide natural adornment for this classic fairy tale wedding."

"I thought Jaza was crazy for wanting the most special day of her life in late October outside in the garden, but this is fabulous."

"My! She has the trellis, the wedding area and the aisle decorated with Calla lilies and cranberries. This is original and elegant. The parents look nice walking in."

"I am glad my mama let Jaza pick out that outfit instead of wearing the one she had purchased. Her dress is beautiful and my mama looks the part with his mom."

"She does. Oh, look, look! She didn't tell us about this! That is Jaza in the glass pumpkin carriage. She's throwing Calla lilies with chocolate colored stems and cranberries to all the guests!"

"She looks like a superstar. This girl has planned this day all of her life. There is our cue – "When You Wish Upon a Star." You have your flowers? Remember to try to drop them down the middle so that she can walk on them"

"Right, we are forming a walkway for her."

As Bonita walked up the aisle to meet Alpine, she had to remind herself that he wasn't hers; he was the best man in the wedding. He looked so handsome and succulent. She could kiss him when the preacher says you may kiss the bride. The poem she wrote to read at the toast she wrote with Alpine in mind. *Come out of your dream, Bonita. Thank God I made it to the altar without falling.*

The audience's response caused Bonita to look to the top of the stairwell on the other side of the garden. Jaza had appeared, looking spectacular. The crystal stones shined rainbows around the room. *Blow me away. Koffer is singing a love lullaby he wrote to Jaza. She didn't know he was going to sing. Don't fall on your big day, girl.*

Jaza bent over the banister and threw him kisses. Bonita couldn't hold back the tears. All the ladies are crying, even Jaza's mama. *This is awesome.*

Koffer's voice was thunderous until Jaza started throwing him kisses, then he became choked up. Jaza reached the gazebo and was lifted up by a hydraulic lift. Bonita's heart dropped as the tears continued to flow down her face when he got on one knee to put on her crystal slippers.

"This is making me weak, I almost dropped the side of you I'm holding up," Bonita whispered into Jaza's ear. "Koffer seems to want to kiss you before it is time."

Jaza was alluring and it was obvious that she had captured the mind of her man and her audience. She leaned over to her man and Bonita heard her say, "I didn't wear panties cause I didn't want them wet." The minister put his head down. Alpine and Bonita both smiled big.

As the minister told Koffer that he may kiss his bride, one hundred white doves were released and bells in the trees were shaken, blowing back and forth and filling the atmosphere with sound.

The wedding distracted Bonita from Alpine, but she could feel him staring through her with radar eyes. When she met his eyes, he didn't look away.

"I'm not sorry, Bonita; I just can't get over your beauty."

"Thank you, Alpine, but I am not the bride."

"You are not the bride yet and I am not talking about your face. I am talking about your heart. Your name means fair, beautiful. I must have missed something before, but I won't miss it again."

"Again. I don't know about again."

The minister called for the receiving line to begin and, all in all, it took about thirty minutes.

"Thank God we took pictures for two weeks prior to the wedding," Bonita said to Carmen and Kate.

"You look pretty, Bonita," Kate said, "But, Jaza is so beautiful. Just over the top gorgeous."

"Yes!" Carmen agreed. "Today, her name should be Bonita. She is Cinderella come to reality."

"The epitome of her fairy tale, she is," Bonita said, in a dreamy voice. "Just what she worked for, or didn't work for." The girls all laughed. "See girls, dreams do come true."

"Hello, Bonita."

The sound of Alpine's voice cause chills to run up her spine. She instantly became nervous and dropped her cup.

"Sorry, Bonita. Hello, ladies. I didn't mean to startle you. I was compelled to come over and express how beautiful you are today. I felt as happy as the groom watching you walk up the aisle. You look like a dream come true."

"We were talking about dreams that come to fruition," Bonita said. She looked around and saw that her friends were gone.

"Have you eaten?"

"No, I haven't since breakfast this morning."

"Would you eat with me?"

"Alpine, what is this? Why –"

Alpine put his finger on my lips. "Shhh... Bonita, I have been watching since rehearsal night, as I walked you to the altar."

"I don't understand you talking."

"I came to the conclusion that you were not going to come over to talk to me, so I figured I'd start it off."

"You are correct. The last conversation I attempted to have with you, you called me a lying murderer."

He put his finger on my lip again. "We are going to enjoy the day, and maybe one another also. We are going to exuberate joy today ." Alpine held Bonita's face in his hands. "I am sorry. I didn't give you the opportunity to explain. I should have listened to you first. I was afraid because I had fallen in love with the Internet girl and I knew that can never be good. But, the reality is that I am the Internet guy." They both smiled.

The Master of Ceremony called attention to the podium; it was time for the families to present the gifts. With pride, the groom's parents announced their gift and gave their blessing. Bonita was proud of Jaza's mama. She spoke eloquently with love and compassion, sharing the joy and peace that she will share eternally with her daughter and new son. She also spoke of the meaning and value of family. Jaza cried loudly and the entire ballroom had tears in their eyes.

Alpine went to get their champagne for the toast and Bonita looked up to see Jean approaching her table with her two kids.

"Hello, Jean," Bonita stood to greet her and to position herself offensively. "Hi, children." She reached down to give them a hug.

"Please don't speak much in front of my children."

"Sister, how are you?" Bonita winked at Jean to cover up for the children.

Jean looked as if she was in pain and after a moment, she said, "I want you to meet my children, Beryl and Shane."

"Hello Beryl and Shane, I am your Auntie Bonita." She hugged each child. "I am glad to finally meet you. We will spend time together and it will be a joy having you around."

"Thank you," Beryl said.

Excited, Shane, "Can you take us out sometimes like Hank's aunt?"

"Stop that, Shane," Jean said.

"Of course! We can do that sometimes soon. Would you like to come, Jean?"

"Hank's mom usually rests when his aunt takes him out."

"Shane," Jean said." Let's get back to our table."

Then, she came close to Bonita to whisper, "This is a little hard for me. After the speech, I think we can both agree that we do need family."

"If we can work as hard at being friends as we did hating one another, we will come through this."

"Yeah."

"Thank you," Bonita said, as she turned to Alpine. "This is my sister, Jean, and her children, Beryl and Shane."

"Hello," he said.

"Hi, we were just getting back to our table," Jean said. "It was nice meeting you."

When they were gone, he said, "I am surprised. You did not tell me you had a sister."

"I feel strange talking to you about this because we are in an estranged relationship. I mean, not only you and me, but my sister and me, also."

Just then, the MC called Alpine and Bonita up together to do their toasts. He took her up to the podium, holding her hand. Hesaid their blessings, Bonita read the poem and then, their toast. When they walked down, everyone clapped and Bonita was embarrassed.

Next was the call for the bridal party to dance with the bride and groom.

"This is the moment I have been waiting for. The dance is slow and the song is called, 'Share My Love'.

Dancing in Alpine's arms, she whispered, "This is unbelievable."

Alpine pulled her close to his body and she was turned on as much as she was the first time they danced. This man was irresistible.

Chapter 19

BONITA REMEMBERED BEING IN a climatic, emotional state that night in the shelter. She sat on the side of her cot in the obscured blackness of the shelter dorm, determined to follow through with her suicide plan when an eerie presence slowly ascended towards her. The cold, dark silence of the night always frightened her, but that night, she sat motionless, thinking that she would not have to do it herself. Potent, odorous body funk overwhelmed her as the presence got closer, however, she sat up, tall fearless and ready to die. A voice came from behind and said, "Whatever ya thinkin', don't do it." The breath of the voice spewed out in blubbery chunks of stink. Jake stood before her, smiling. She looked between the spaces of his few rotten teeth and saw desperation. *He has not risked entering the women's quarter to kill me,* she thought, as her heart sunk.

"We need you here. We love you."

Passion poured from his heart. And tears fell from Bonita's eyes. No one had ever wanted her without reason. "You can make it. You doin' it for us and you. We watch you every day and me and da boys follow you to safety." Then, he hugged her and either the stench or the love served as an anesthetic for her.

"You gave some of these people in here courage and hope they didn't have fa years. Please don't do that ta yourself 'cause you would be killin' the inside of all of us. Jus take a deep breath. Ya can climb this mountain."

Jake tipped his ragged hat and walked off. She looked around the room and eyes were peeping out from the covers. *How did they know my thoughts? I had always ignored him, thought of him and the others here, especially his friend, as low lifes, good for nothing vagrants and damn, he saved my life. He was the one that snatched me from the hands of death. Umh! I wonder where is Jake today?*

Bonita looked through her thoughts from a chair in the sun room to watch the sunshine fall through the raindrops. Glistening light reflected from the sun and the rain as her mind drifted in and out across the memories of life. Looking for love in all the wrong places, she couldn't' imagine who would have thought of such a phrase. Where could the wrong place for love be? Love can be found anywhere. When she thought about it, she realized that she had found most of her love in unlikely places.

Some of the unnecessary situations she had found herself in had been horrific, but the gift of wisdom and understanding in the aftermath was the reward. She knew that she was much richer for having traveled the dark and dreary road that brought forth the rainbow and the pot of gold at the end of it. The night Jake came into the ladies dorm, she had planned the perfect suicide. Her pride could not handle facing her mom as a failure and that held her from making the phone call that would have rescued her. Bonita thought it was pride that had stopped her from calling her mom often. However, she ultimately realized that it was fate that had kept her from her life's treasures.

It seemed as though her head was spinning like the earth on its axis. Sometimes, her inner being made her feel like she was on a merry-go-round, spinning faster and faster. It is sickening, but so good. She had decided not to make any decisions for her life at this time; she wanted to just live, at this point. And it was supper. She remembered when she felt like her circulatory system had become overgrown with mold and mildew. *You must have given me antifungal from heaven. I am glad you were not my magic man producing at my every command. I have received much love from the hopeless and the homeless. They are who directed me to the real you. That's good too.*

It would be nice to know the truth about life. What are life's truths, she wondered. Most times, the truth can't be handled. She most likely could not handle any more truth that day. If she had seen the future beforehand, she would have never thought that she could handle the truths that had occurred in her life and would have made a meticulous effort to avert them. Most of the truth would have been murderous lies and the devil's perceptions would have been her thoughts. She would have cursed the devil repeatedly. The horrible truths life presented her caused her to see her own fallibility as potting soil for the compassionate heart that she had attained from this hell fire experience. She didn't know why, but she had a peace about it.

Bonita would have never thought that low-down Jake was watching anybody or cared about anything. She remembered the night Carrie had walked up to her with her usual filthy, dirty, muddy "white" shoes and rotten teeth, looking like she was expecting her to fix her world. I didn't want to know her. She took a seat and went on to exclaim, "Jake didn't make it in last night. They found him frozen on the street and took him to the state hospital. Nobody knows if he is going to make it. We don't know how to find out." Bonita took a few deep breath and realized that she had cared about Jake. He had saved her life. It seemed that all the regulars in the shelter were a tight knit family. Carrie was the one voted to come to Bonita for answers about Jake. They counted on her. She was considered a part of the family. She said they watched her get beautiful every morning. She asked Bonita if she was afraid.

"Yes," Bonita admitted. "I'm afraid."

The hurt on Carrie's face startled her. Bonita then told her that she was working and had saved enough money to move into her own place. Carrie looked sad, but Bonita also saw that there was some excitement in her expression. Carrie suddenly became serious and she put her head down.

"Us homeless people are not bad, poor thieves and drug addicts. As a matter of fact, Jake has money. There are nights when he pays for all of us to sleep here. Some of us get checks and have good sponsors who take care of our needs. For others, like Red, sponsors are leeches that take their money and give them next to nothing every month. Out here on our side of this jungle, the haves take care of the have-nots. Some of us spent many years paying taxes and taking care of America." Carrie spoke adamantly and Bonita felt ashamed.

She spoke with pride until Bonita asked her what her story was. She hung her head and tears began to fall from her eyes. As Bonita wiped the tears from Carrie's eyes, she told her story.

She had been a supervisor at the United States Post Office. Her husband had an affair with a twenty-two year old woman, who was actually her baby sister from her mother's third marriage. He convinced her children and the courts that she was insane, had her committed, took the children, the family's savings and never looked back for her. When she found out that she had lost everything, had no place to go and could not get a job because she had been declared mentally incapable, all that she decided she could do was play the part. She found this family when she was released from the mental institution and refused to leave them.

"I'm safe here," she said. "I don't want the responsibility of taking care of myself again. If anything happens to Jake, I don't know what we will do. I went over to the hospital to take care of Jake for the next fourteen days and gave report to the family nightly.

"Then, there was Nikki. She would come into the shelter on the nights her husband panhandled the money for her and the two girls to sleep in the shelter. He and the boys slept on the streets every night. I believe the friends I met in the home had more integrity that most people I've met, the "haves," as they are called in the family."

Sitting reflecting on the times she had spent in the shelter and the people she'd met, she realized that she didn't have friends that could compare to Jake and the family. They cared after her when she despised them and called them low-life vagrants. She hated their existence before she had gotten to know them, yet she was one of them. They all laid there in the shelter every night like hurt, damaged, scary puppies. They were like animals made lame by the big hits of life. They couldn't see the beauty of who they were because they were blinded by their vague existence that distorted their realities. This was Bonita's realization.

It was a good thing that she had gotten to know Carrie and the crew and nursed Jake back to health before she had met Kate. Instead of being blinded by her addiction and pain, she was able to see the beautiful, budding flower that needed to be watered and cared for. She saw the true Kate through the eyes of the family's love. She was one of her most precious relationships. Having Kate as a friend was valuable to her and she wouldn't want to be without her.

I think I'll tell her that, Bonita decided.

Mr. Thomas promoted Bonita to her one-room apartment called "On My Way." One day, on her way home, she looked down at a woman who was calling to her. She was literally crawling on the ground and she looked up to ask her for something to eat. Bonita helped her up and took her home. When she got her in, she bathed her and hand fed her bread, eggs and milk. Bonita knew it had taken courage to continue the daily fight for life. She and the family encouraged Kate continuously. That is what made it difficult putting her on the street every day whenever Bonita left for work. By the time Mr. Thomas

discovered she had a roommate in her little box, she had already pro-
gressed to volunteer work. The family vouched for her and he didn't
have the heart to evict Bonita and her new roommate.

*Oh Lord, the more I sit here reminiscing on the past, the more I see
You all over our lives. We were all left for dead and You gave us life, in
spite of ourselves.* Every moment was painful, but enriching.

҂

Bonita believed that the relationship between her and Jaza would
be restored after their falling out. Jaza brought humanism back to
her world. She was a person who Bonita could trust with a relationship. Jaza was a lonely girl, surfing the Internet for a man. But, it was
the conversations about her life, self-love and joy from within that
brought Bonita and her friends together. Jaza may not have been a
great worker, but she was a great friend. Bonita came to despise being
her boss, but she understood that the growth that had come out of
the situation was worth the pain. Standing firm against the negative
qualities of a friend brings them deeper into a solid truth that cannot
be refused. The lie would have to be rejected by the heart to make
room for the truth that builds character. There was nothing else to
do. The pain of feeling betrayed killed the lining of her spirit and being accused of being a Judas was bruising to her heart. But, all of that
was priceless when compared to becoming treasures. Bonita knew
that if she had the chance to do it all over, she'd do it all again.

҂

"Hello, Jaza I was just thinking about you," Bonita said, answering the
phone. "You are on your honeymoon, why are you calling me?"

"Koffer is out playing golf. I called to say thank you."

"Ok then, you're welcome. I imagined on a honeymoon, the married people would be glued together. He's playing golf?"

"Get out of the fantasy for a minute. We are enjoying one another and are having a great time. On your honeymoon, you choose a place that has attractions both of you are interested in together and alone. This is the most important time to be yourself."

"I guess we would both need time to breathe right. Are you happy?"

"I am rich in joy. The Internet paid off."

"For both of us right. I think my relationship with Alpine might be going somewhere. Our dates are good. We are enjoying one another again. I would have never thought I would be with an Internet man named Alpine. Where did his mom get that name?"

"I don't care about his name. I am so glad you have someone in your life other than the old people in the home."

"You know, it feels so good to finally go out to dinner as the woman with a man. I know what the ladies are thinking as we pass by. I am so happy that is not me anymore. Cheerios to you, Lord. Have a good time; I will hang up so that you can enjoy your honeymoon."

"Not before I say what I have called to say," Jaza said.

"Ok."

"I want to thank you for being an intricate part of my growth into womanhood. I thank you for accepting only the best from me. It has caused me to face all truth within myself. I have had to face things that I didn't like and transform her into a queen who functions in the beauty of integrity and honesty. This woman is profitable to me, my husband and my family. I am proud of her. I thank you for calling this woman from the inside of me."

"Aw, don't make me cry. That is because I know what you have done for me. I could only relate to her, the deep inner soul of the righteous person you are. Pretty girls sometimes get trapped in the place where you were. I love you, Jaza, and thank you."

"I love you, Bonita."

They both said goodbye to each other.

Wow, she thought of me on her honeymoon. I feel so special. Feeling alone was an empty lie I convinced myself to see as the truth.

The phone rang again and she answered.

"Hello?"

"Hello. Are you taking care of my only baby?"

"Mommy, just as you taught me to. How is your day?"

"I did visit Auntie Eva. She had the audacity to speak of my single daughter and asked if there was a wedding in the dismal future or would you miss the family reunion again. We bantered about our single daughters for few minutes."

"Mom, I'm dating."

"You do exude joy. I am enthralled!"

"It is real what you sense, Mother. I have been dating him since Jaza's wedding."

"Is it Alpine? His family delved deep to get that name."

"He is a wonderful guy. Chivalry is not dead. He opens doors for me, speaks to the waiter, is always on time, brings flowers and calls just to say 'hello, I'm thinking of you'."

"That is a good start. Does he pray? Is he the marrying kind? Does he want children in the future?"

"He has invited me to church with his family and it was a blessed occasion. He does want a wife and a family. He says it was love at first sight. He doesn't need time to tell him that I am the woman God created for him."

"Yes, I am so happy for you. I hope you marry before Joleen. Auntie Eva cannot have grandchildren prior to me becoming a grandmother."

Bonita laughed loudly. "Mom, how is the guy you met?"

"He divorced his wife. I saw the papers."

"Mom, you should marry him. I want you to have your own husband. You deserve a mate. You are beautiful."

"You have mentioned beautiful, how do you dress to go out on dates?"

"Well, first of all, I apply make up to accentuate my beautiful eyes."

"Eyes like your father."

"Mom, I choose my wardrobe like the queen that I am. One night, he said, 'You are so beautiful, I am afraid to touch you'."

"I am ecstatic!"

"And when he kissed me, Mom, it was like magic. It was eternal. I spoke softly to him, like dew on the morning grass and I said, 'Now that was a kiss to keep'."